CATHY COME HOME

By the same author

EDNA, THE INEBRIATE WOMAN

DOWN AND OUT IN BRITAIN

SYNTHETIC FUN

GYPSIES

IN SEARCH OF THE MAGIC MUSHROOM

TOMORROW'S PEOPLE

SMILING DAVID

PROSTITUTES

CATHY COME HOME

by

JEREMY SANDFORD

Marion Boyars
London

A MARION BOYARS BOOK
distributed by
Calder & Boyars Ltd
18 Brewer Street, London W1R 4AS

First published in Great Britain in 1976
by Marion Boyars Publishers Ltd
18 Brewer Street, London W1R 4AS

ISBN 0 7145 2515 4 Cased edition
ISBN 0 7145 2516 2 Paperback edition

Typesetting by Gilbert Composing Services,
Leighton Buzzard, Beds.

Printed by Unwin Brothers Limited,
Gresham Press, Old Woking, Surrey.
A member of the Staples Printing Group.

CONTENTS

INTRODUCTION

(adapted from a tape-recorded interview with Alan Rosenthal)

In the early sixties I was living in Battersea in a poor district and one day a neighbour of mine was evicted. The family's furniture was thrown out into the street, and they disappeared, apparently without trace. They had nowhere to go, and I wondered what had become of them. A few nights later a friend came to tell me that this neighbour had arrived in a place which was more disgusting and more frightful than one could possibly imagine.

These were the days before anyone outside bureaucratic circles had ever heard such phrases as 'Part III Accommodation' or 'Emergency Housing for the Homeless', and 'Homeless Family' had not become part of the jargon of sociologists and newspaper men. What I found when I went to visit my former neighbour both angered and saddened me. It was a scene of horror, all the worse for the fact that no one knew about it.

Hundreds of families were stacked into an old workhouse. Mothers and children separated from their husbands and fathers, occupying a single room each or, in some cases, four or five or more families all shoved into the same room. The toilet facilities were completely inadequate and dysentery was rife. Ambulances called every day, and more than once a day. There was a feeling of complete demoralisation. Husbands were allowed to visit their wives and children only for a couple of hours each night. In the afternoon, even when it was raining, mothers and children were forced out into the streets. They weren't allowed to remain indoors. The reason given for this was that they were meant to be finding accommodation; this was impossible. Obviously, they would hardly be here in these horrible conditions if they hadn't tried to the end of their ability to find accommodation elsewhere. Feeding was communal and some of the mothers, fearing that their children would catch dysentery, forbade their children to eat. Ultimately hunger would prevail. They would eat–and become diseased. It was rare to find a mother here who had not once had her child down with dysentery. For the privilege of living here here these families paid quite a high rent, a fact which further aggravated their difficulties. Since the husband's wages were being used up in this way, and also in travel coming to see their families, there was no money to pay for outside accommodation, even if they were able to find it. The situation was then, as it still is: for a man at the lower end of the wage bracket in the big industrial centres, it was very hard indeed to find accommodation at a price that he could afford. At that time there were a few thousand British people in this situation. The heartbreak of mothers and children unwillingly separated from their husbands and fathers was a terrible thing to see. Added to the heartbreak of disease and the shame of being in these places was a further humiliation. On arrival, all families were made to sign a document in which they stated that they clearly understood that the accommodation was only 'Emergency Accommodation'. They were only there on sufferance–they must make constant attempts to find other housing and if they had not done this by the end of three months, they would be turned out even from the Home for the Homeless. In practice, this rule was not followed. The numbers of homeless packed into these old workhouses continued to rise, many staying past the three month limit. Families were still there after a year or even two years, but at the end of the line there still came the moment when homeless families were told—'You can't stay here any longer'. At this point, the mother, knowing what lay ahead, would become frantic. Often by now the husbands, ashamed, humiliated, and unable to cope with the situation, would have abandoned their families anyway. This is no slur on the husbands, but it is a slur on the situation which society had provided for them. The frantic women would redouble their efforts to find accommodation, but in their demoralised state, they were in no fit condition of mind to find it, even if it were available. Then a brutal letter would arrive to inform them that they must vacate their quarters in the Home for the Homeless. I remember being with one such mother when she received this letter. She was living in an almost incredible building, in which thirty homeless families were housed in a vast chamber, along the sides of which were stable-like stalls with wooden walls about five feet high, and only flimsy curtains across the front. There was no roof. This is where these families ate, slept, lived—one in each stall. She knew what the letter meant. She knew that when she was evicted the children would be taken away from her and put into care. I learned at this time it was happening to something like twenty-one children per week in the London area alone. I felt that conditions so vile should immediately be brought to the attention of the public. To my surprise, when I asked whether any of them had approached any newspaper, I was told that a large number had in fact written letters, but these had been ignored or sent back with polite but evasive replies. At this time, 'the Homeless' were not news. My immediate reaction was to ask whether I might do a programme on BBC Sound Radio about these homeless Families. I did it with a neighbour of mine, Heather Sutton, who had first brought my attention to this situation. It consisted of recordings made of those who actually were homeless, which we interspersed with what struck me as the somewhat bland and heartless explanations of those who had the job of looking after them. These recordings were made in Part III Accommodation, with the knowledge of the LCC. They permitted us to record in what I suppose was the best of all the accommodation in which homeless families were being kept.

The reason they didn't allow us to go to the worst places—the Reception Centres—was that they said the homeless would be in too distraught a state of mind to be able to give an objective picture. The accommodation in the place they allowed us to go, Durham Buildings, was unpleasant, but not nearly so nasty as that at Newington Lodge, the place I had originally visited. However, all the families in Durham Buildings had passed through Newington Lodge, and the experience had scarred them. They seemed unable to forget it, and even while talking of the present, they spoke of the experiences they had had there in the past. Even in Durham Buildings they still felt insecure. The men here were allowed back with their families, but a sense of shame lingered. There was hostility from local shopkeepers. One man said: 'I was a prisoner of war and I spent five years behind the wire fighting for this country, and I still feel I'm a prisoner. I've never had a place of my own where I could do what I like'.

We went to Newington Lodge, and made some recordings there, illegally, and also to the place with the stable-like stalls. Here the pressure, indeed sheer bloody-mindedness of the staff, seemed to have created a different picture. People were terrified of talking to us for fear that the authorities might hear about it, and this would tell against them, and they would be evicted. As a result of some articles in the local paper, so they claimed, three women and their children had been thrown out because it was thought that they'd spoken to the man who wrote the articles. The fear of these pathetic people was a horrible thing to see. Realising that we were an embarrassment to them, we didn't choose to stay too long.

One girl at Newington Lodge became my friend. She thought the conditions there must be exposed and was willing to risk being thrown out in the interests of others.

The reaction to the radio programme *Homeless Families* was absolutely nil. I had the impression, as so often when working for radio, of shouting something important down a deep well. I returned to Newington Lodge later with the *Observer* cameraman, Donald McCullin and, although photographs were forbidden in the building by the LCC, we were able to take some photographs with the help of our friend. Suddenly, the word flashed along the corridor. 'The Warden is coming', and we hid under the bed. Later the police were called and we were charged with being in illegal possession of our own cameras and tape recorder. We were taken to the local police station, where we were kept for much of the night before being able to establish the real nature of our quest. I imagine that this was a put-up job demonstrating that our police force are sometimes forgetful of their duty to be impartial and make the mistake of siding (rather too much) with those who run these institutions.

I wrote *Cathy* the same way I do most of my writing. I filled a hard-backed spring binder with bits of quarto paper which had the headings of the various sections of the film on them, such as caravan, slum, luxury flat, mother in law, courting, the first Home for the Homeless the second Home for the Homeless. Then I worked from a very large number of newspaper clippings that I had accumulated through the years, transcripts of tape recordings, actual tape recordings, notes of people I had met, and places I had been to—picking them out at random, seeing if they fitted what I wanted to do or not. Most of them I rejected, but those which seemed to fit, I included, sometimes in altered form, sometimes almost verbatim. This went on for a couple of months.

Having written a large number of little scenes like this for each section I juggled them around in the best order, and then I had it typed.

The story went through my typist two or three times after that. Each time I worked through it, trying to see it with objective eyes, excluding some scenes, altering the position of others, amplifying, writing a few new scenes out of my head and adding new touches to Cathy's character or things that occurred to me as I went along—the general drudge which I expect many writers go through, working on and on at a script until it is right.

I did all this over a period of three or four months. I often work at an office or some small room away from home, and at this time I had a delightful, very small attic room, high up at the back of a pleasant house in Oakley Street, Chelsea. I was able to scatter papers everywhere in deep piles like snow and, I was going to say, enjoy myself. But in fact writing *Cathy* was a very gruelling experience and, although I had a feeling of immense satisfaction and fulfilment, I often finished the day feeling more dead than alive, since I had never tackled so large or serious a subject before.

I had thought there would be buyers for *Cathy* but there were none. I had a first-rate director wanting to do it, and, I thought, a powerful script, but there were no buyers.

So, for a year and a half I worked at other things, periodically pushing *Cathy* in all sorts of directions. In the end, I became so doubtful of anybody buying it, that I decided to write it as a book, so that it could have a life after all.

About halfway through the transformation into the

book, Tony Garnett, a BBC producer whom I had never met, rang me to say that he had found my synopsis at the bottom of the BBC TV Wednesday play filing cabinets, was very enthusiastic about it, and would like Ken Loach to direct it.

So *Cathy* became famous.

We met for lunch in the BBC canteen, and I explained about the play's previous history of refusals, thinking that this would put him off. It didn't. We did resolve, however, to keep the play's subject very secret and, to give it for the moment a different title and, if anybody should ask us, to refer to it as a knock-about family comedy, which it was in a way except for the comedy bit. The director, Ken Loach, has a wonderful gift for simplification and he made many suggestions at this point; the effect was to give the story a more simplified or 'classical' shape. The major suggestions which he made and to which I agreed, were in the opening section of the film. I had gone at far greater length into Cathy's arrival in London.

Looking back on it, there are two points I'd like to make.

People often tell me that Cathy was too attractive—a girl as attractive as that could never have become homeless. This is nonsense. I would say that, on average, the girls I've met in Part III Accommodation were more attractive than those outside, although I couldn't say why.

Secondly, people tell me that all the things that happened to Cathy could not have happened to one girl. This is also nonsense. A newspaper once sent out fifty reporters to seek out Britain's 'true-life Cathys'. The stories they sent back were, without exception, far more complicated than Cathy's. There were many more changes of addresses. A few, though not most, fought ferociously for their children before they were taken from them.

I wish that there had been more change in the general situtation of Britain's Homeless since I wrote *Cathy*. As regards its particular effect, however, I can feel pleased. It is good to know that I have altered, if only by a very small bit, the condition of life for others in my own society. As a result of the film and certain meetings we held in Birmingham afterwards, this town, and others, ceased their practice of separating three or four hundred husbands each year from their wives and children. The husbands were allowed to return back to their families in a great gushing stream. It was intensely moving. I was lucky enough to be present on this jubilant occasion, and that moment, if no other, justified in my opinion not only my writing of *Cathy* but also my own existence.

Jeremy Sandford

CREDITS

Written by	Jeremy Sandford
Director	Kenneth Loach
Photography	Tony Imie
Sound	Malcolm Campbell
Editor	Roy Watts
Producer	Tony Garnett

Cathy Come Home was written in late 1963 and early 1964. It was filmed by Kenneth Loach for the BBC in summer 1966 and first transmitted later that year.

The version of the script printed here is the Script from which the film was made (BBC 1, 2116/4369). I have added two scenes which were not in this script but were improvised (one is the 'Christine Rowbottom' scene); and have tidied it up in various ways to make it easier reading. I have also added some of the voices that were heard on wildtrack in the course of the film. Much of this wildtrack consisted of the words of real people living in the various locations we shot. I tape-recorded them, and here include about half of those that were used in the film.

CAST

CATHY	Carol White
REG	Ray Brooks
MRS WARD (Senr.)	Winifred Dennis
PROPERTY AGENTS	Geoffrey Palmer Gillian Paterson
GRANDAD	Wally Patch
WELFARE OFFICER	Gabrielle Hamilton
LORRY DRIVER	Eric Mason
HOUSING OFFICER	John Baddeley
MR HODGE	Frank Veasey
	James Benton
MRS ALLEY	Phyllis Hickson
	Barry Jackson
IN COURT	Ruth Kettlewell Kathleen Broadhurst Emmett Hennessey
	Alec Coleman Ralph Lawton
IN THE CARAVANS	Gladys Dawson Ronald Pember Paddy Joyce Maureen Ampleford Reg Lye Liz McKenzie Henry Kay Anne Ayres
THE RATEPAYERS	Leonard Pearce David Crane Alan Selwyn
SLEEPING ROUGH	Will Stampe Geraldine Moon Bernard Price

AT CUMBERMERE LODGE	
STAFF	Charles Leno John Lawrence Joan Harsant Faith Kent
INMATES	Julie May Myrtle McKenzie Patti Dalton Rose Hiller Paddy Kent Edwin Brown Helen Booth Lila Kaye Anne Hardcastle
AT HOLM LEA	Cleo Sylvester Terri Ansell Andrea Lawrence Doreen Herrington Muriel Hunte

The author expresses deep and sincere thanks to Tony Garnett as producer, to Ken Loach as director, and to Carol White for her unsurpassable performance as Cathy.

Incredible though it may seem, the whole film, more complicated than many a feature film, was shot in less than three weeks.

Strong pressure was put on the establishment of the BBC to recant, to 'confess' that the picture given was inaccurate, to apologise. It is greatly to the credit of three men in particular that they stood by the film. The men were Sidney Newman, head of Drama Group; Kenneth Adam, Director of Television; and Hugh Greene, Director General.

CATHY COME HOME

screenplay

A YOUNG GIRL *stands by the entrance to the motorway, waiting for a lift.*

She shifts from one foot to the other, walks a little, impeded by her 'smart' shoes, turns round as lorries or cars pass.

She's evidently been left here by another car that brought her this far. She's young, pretty, and with an air of excitement about her; freed at last from ties to her family, heart-whole, at the age of consent, but unconsenting as yet, exultant yet shy. She carries a change of clothes, shoes, etc. in a parcel.

With a hiss of its steam brakes a lorry draws to a stop ahead of her.

CATHY *moves towards it. The door swings open; the* DRIVER *leans out.*

DRIVER. Well, well, well, where we going then? Touring?

CATHY. Where *you* going?

DRIVER. Motorway.

She looks him over a moment, friendly, yet shy, then says, reckless, trusting him;

CATHY. O.K.

She climbs in, inexpertly, throwing her parcel up first. The door shuts. The lorry begins to move off.

We see CATHY *through windscreen, as she gazes ahead, trees, hills, reflected in windscreen, and the* DRIVER *glances at her as the lorry gains speed, sizing her up.*

We hear the voice of;

CATHY. Well, I *was* a bit fed up . . . didn't seem to be much there for me . . . you know how these little towns are . . . *one* coffee bar . . . it was closed on a Sunday.

The DRIVER *is respecting* CATHY'S *silence, but liking her;*

DRIVER. Was you by any chance interested in music?

The DRIVER *leans to switch on the lorry radio, so that we have tinny music for the journey as it continues.*

We hear the voice of;

CATHY. . . . didn't even tell them I was going . . . I sent them a card when I got down there . . .

The lorry approaches the big city. The lorry passes through subtopia and the dingy down town area, which is to be CATHY'S *home; the city with its hopes, heartlessness, excitement, squalor.*

CATHY. That house over there . . . that one with the broken steps, that's where I went for the room, and the fella tried to practically rape me! . . . Where did I get a room in the end? Oh, yeah, down there, Mantua Street. Three pound a week.

They pass a garage.

That's where I got my first job–petrol pump girl . . . I was mad in a way in those days . . .

suppose you could say I was bored, wanted a bit of adventure . . . some adventure.

By an urban stream, half stream, half sewer

REG *and* CATHY *are walking.*

REG. They're all travellin in hearses, you see Cath, to this what they call unusual supper party. Then the chandelier falls on him don't it, he's strangled with diamonds. And she that's grown to forty foot high—

CATHY. You mean through the radio active dust.

REG. Yes, that's right. She stretches her hand in down through the winda (when she's come howling over the endless desert), she picks up the mean blonde piece he's been doing it with, they're jitterbugging (it's quite an old film, see) and she holds this blonde up in the palm of her massive hand. And the man jumps up for her, dinny, e wants to get at er, don't e. But unbeknownst to her, see, there's been some swapping around, it's not her husband no more. And the fella's mask slips off, that's trying to get at her, and who d'you think it really is? Dracula.

CATHY. Horror films used to send me, when I was fifteen. But, funny, now I only like sex films.

Now we see REG *and* CATH *under some trees, embrace.*

We hear the voice of;

CATHY. When I come up to town I thought I knew all the answers. Silly ant I. Gone and got myself involved with you.

Down the sewer/stream iceberg white mounds of detergent float slowly on towards the river.

REG. By the way, Cath, I'd like to kiss you again, Cath . . .

In the Centre of Town

CATHY. Nice, enit. Have to walk up the street with you like a rotten old sod.

REG. Rotten old sod? You should be proud of me!

CATHY. Proud! Nice enit, seen with someone like that, in a shoddy pair of trousers.

REG *laughs.*

CATHY. Out of the ark. Nice enit. Don't laugh neither, you wait.

REG. Wait for what?

CATHY. You wait! I tramped on that hat I didn't like, didn't I? Well, I'll trample on something else and all. I'll trample your trousers an you aint careful. Trample em up.

REG. Should think a girl like you got better things to do.

CATHY. Better things! An if I have, not with you.

REG. Get stuffed.

CATHY *after a short pause, sultry;*

CATHY. You wait!

As they continue to walk we hear the voice of;

CATHY. And even when he did buy new things they looked all wrong on him. He would get them slim

Jim ties. Then he got them trousers with the stitched in golden seams . . . oh Gawd . . . I never seen nothing like it . . .

In the Cabin of a Lorry

CATHY *and* REG *driving.*

CATHY. But won't you get into trouble. Taking me with you?

REG. Trouble? Never! No Cath, that's the advantage of working for a small firm see, like this one. They're not particular. Listen, whatever your hours, whether you get your stamps, whether you flog yourself to death or take it easy, see, they don't care. If you give a lift to any bird, they don't care. They ain't particular.

CATHY. Oh, so this isn't the first time you've given a bird a lift?

REG. Now, don't be silly.

They are in a totter's yard.

CATHY. Why don't you find someone else to go out with? I mean, you don't always have to go out with me. How d'you know, you might find someone that you like better.

REG. I won't find no one I like better.

CATHY. But how do you know though?

REG. Look, do you mind. I've had a few bints in my time. I happen to like you the best.

He leads her past lorries, behind old bedsteads and wardrobes and stacks of iron and piles of old ledgers and sacks containing the stuffing taken out of cushions and compressed tins, old radiators, sofas, and bits of pianos, where amongst these an old rusty fire escape tilts up towards the sky. He takes her hand and leads her up it.

CATHY. Is it safe?

REG. Course it is. Now, you can see a bit already. Look. You can see half the town from here. Nearly.

They continue up past the brown masonry, following the iron staircase upwards.

CATHY. Reg! It's falling! It's going to fall!

She cowers back against the windowsill.

REG. It's all right Cath, it's not falling.

CATHY. No! Reg!

She seems paralysed with fear.

REG. Come on. Now. Let me help you. There.

He gets ahead of her onto the parapet and pulls her up.

CATHY'S *momentum carries her on and* REG *catches her in his arms.*

CATHY. Trust you!

It's filthy dirty up here, chimneys and old roofs, old brown bricks standing up drunkenly into the sky.

CATHY. Trust you to bring me up to a rotten old place like this. How we goin to get down?

REG. Don't worry! Live in the present, eh Cath?

He picks up a brick from the top of the parapet. Throws it. There is a crashing sound from below.

REG. Rotten enit. This whole place'll be down before long.

CATHY. I was frightened, Reg. I ant got much courage.

Later, REG *says;*

REG. I reckon it's just us now, enit. Just us. Just you and me eh?

CATHY. I wouldn't mind.

REG. Have some kiddies, eh Cath?

CATHY. I'd like that.

REG. Sod to all the rest.

In a Pub

REG. . . . Three inches long, and they flies with a heavy vibrating sound. They was first noticed soon after the war. Workmen rebuilding the toilet was set upon by the vibration beetles. They was routed entirely, you see, they were council workmen they were . . .

The wedding reception is in full swing.

REG, *by now rather dishevelled and* CATHY *in white.*

REG. . . .Then came the sanitary man, that they call the health doodah. He perceives that the beetles are resident in a scrapped up tree at the back of May's Caf. They threw disinfectant into the tree. It got in May's dinner and killed two. The beetles got worse. So then they pull down the old air raid shelter, and built up on top ten stories of flats. That ought to kill em, they reckon. But no! The beetles are worse than ever. They cluster about the street lamps! They sit on the washing! So Mum, she put some into a box, took em up to the housing chief. When she got there, she emptied em out on his desk! The beetles got into the minutes. They ate up all the bleeding minutes! So, bottoms up and keep your windows shut.

GRANDAD. *Friendly.* And keep your bloody gob shut!

REG. You can't speak to me like that on me bloody wedding day. I'm a man of stature I am!

VOICE. Statue! You'll be standin up straight, tonight.

VOICE. Dirty slob!

We hear other snatches of conversation:

JOHNNY. Things has changed. Remember when we was thirteen, fourteen, used to go down the park, there was birds everywhere. Like under every tree. They've gone now. You don't find em there now. Where do they go now? They all go down the Palais.

RAY. Your turn now, Eil.

EILEEN. Never. Not me.

RAY. Why not?

EILEEN. I'll never give in I'd rather make the fellas wild.

MAY. *Adenoidal.* My husband always said he'd fit it up and sell it. Reckoned he'd get thirty quid for it. Now I don't think he'd get a penny.

MAVIS. What's wrong with it then?

MAY. *Gaily.* It has no seats.

LOTTIE. Huh. Huh. Huh. Huh.

MAY. No headlamps.

LOTTIE. Huh. Huh. Huh. Huh.

MAY. No ceiling.

LOTTIE. Huh, Huh. No wheels?

MAY. No wheels

LOTTIE. No nought?

MAY. No nought.

DENNIS BROACHER. Totter means scrounger, in other words he won't pay for a thing he'll scrounge it. Say there's an old bedstead in your backyard, your totter will scrounge it. As opposed to the general dealer, as for example meself. A general dealer is on the level, he's quite a different matter.

REG'S MUM. *To* CATHY. It's a good day for the

family, Reg getting engaged to a girl like you. No, straight. I was sayin to Charlie–You see this family really has come down in the world. I spect you can see that. Charlie hasn't always been like he is now. Oh no. Once he did a big deal. *To* CHARLIE, *she shouts:* Didn't you Charlie? *To* CATHY: He can't hear. Concerning three thousand chairs. Yes, *three thousand chairs.* So as a result we went to live in Devon and we did in ever such a nice posh chalet.

REG'S DAD, *who's overheard, now joins in the conversation;*

REG'S DAD. Pish posh, ever such a lovely tip top pish posh chalet.

REG'S MUM. You're sloshed! All with multi-tone decor. So anyway, what d'you think happened? Would you believe it. We was ignored. Flat! We reckoned it was because the neighbours was on the crooked.

GRANDAD *makes voilent conspiratorial gestures to* CATHY.

GRANDAD. Listen, you may not know it, but I'm a composer I am. You know 'Misty Morning'? That's the signature tune for Charlie Forsyte? I wrote that. But I never got no credit. 'Coming to the End of Love'. I wrote that too. But never got no credit. The thing is down in Devon, there where we used to be living, we were in a boarding house, there was the old pianna standin in the corner, they'd say, 'Come on old Charlie, give us one of your compositions!' So I'd be playin away, trillin away like this;

He makes elaborate trilling gestures

Trilling away, not a thought in me head, trilling and trilling not thinking–course, unbeknownst to me there was this fella sitting at the back all the time, writing it all down!

REG'S MUM. Ours is a healthy house, ours is, thirteen living here and never a death. Hey, you're from the country parts ent you? Anyway, what's it like out there in the country places?

CATHY. Oh, it's all right. Bit boring. Well, really it's horrible. Compared to this. Well, there was nothing for me. Ow! *She yells.* Reg!

REG'S MUM. Hey, what's that for?

CATHY. You would of and all if you knew what he did to me! Only put a olive down the back of me neck!

Reg's Mum's Place

The WELFARE OFFICER *is talking to* GRANDAD. REG'S MUM *is there.*

WELFARE OFFICER. And a slight history of incontinence.

REG'S MUM. Yes, there is that.

GRANDAD *sits up very straight. This is an ordeal for him.*

WELFARE OFFICER. Rambling in his mind at all? Find it hard to remember the odd little thing?

REG'S MUM. *Indulgent.* A little, arn't you grandad?

WELFARE OFFICER. And has to be helped with dressing?

He consults his notes.

WELFARE OFFICER. Well, yes, there would certainly appear to be a case for, er, your father going into care. What do you feel about it, Grandad?

GRANDAD. Well–if you ask me–

REG'S MUM. In addition though, there is the fact that we need the space. Yes. There's the two boys, see. They're coming back out of the army, so we just can't keep him. And they say at the council, it's statutary overcrowding. Eh, Grandad?

WELFARE OFFICER. Yes, of course.

REG'S MUM. *Aside.* The incontinence is getting pretty bad.

WELFARE OFFICER. Well, Grandad, you'll be in one of our larger homes, Rivermeade, I expect you may have seen it! Up by the Town Hall. It's especially suitable for you in that it has facilities on offer of all sorts that might not be available in a smaller place. In addition to this, you'll find that there's always plenty going on, plenty to keep the time passing, what with dances and hobby clubs of various sorts. And there is help available for things that may be getting a little complicated, like dressing and attention to your feet.

In a Luxury Flat

As REG *moves furniture around, hangs up curtains, we hear the voice of;*

CATHY. Funny how a place like this smells different. Must be the central heating. Feels different too. In your bones. Oh, what a place! Fitted carpets, tin openers fixed to the wall, double glazing. And the neighbours. Talk about stylish.

REG. Yeah, see, you put all your rubbish down 'ere, it

goes down the shute at this end, it comes out down there.

CATHY. Look, that's good. What's that Reg?

REG. Double windows, so's the sounds of the traffic don't disturb you. And so it keeps the heat in.

REG *hangs up a picture called 'Elephants at Ambasila'.*

CATHY. Yeah, but Reg, can we really afford this place?

REG. Course we can. Bit late now when we've taken it.

CATHY. No, but there's no point in having such a posh place if we can't afford it. Look, you're earning twenty a week, is it?

REG. Twenty? Twenty-five. Course we can afford it—what; I'm earning twenty-five and you, what is it, six plus three in tips—well, what does that make? Thirty-five quid? We're bloody millionaires. Gawd, course we can run to a penthouse apartment

costing ten a week.

CATHY. Are we worth thirty-five a week?

In the Shops

We see them in the shops enjoying choice, enjoying affluence. Music, as CATHY *wanders round in a happy dream, feathering her nest. And* OTHER SALESMEN'S VOICES *break in saying;*

SALESMEN. Are you being served, sir? Can I help you madam?

In the Luxury Flat

REG. Cathy, what's wrong? You look *bad*

CATHY. No, I'm all right. Just, you know, you go out and when you get back you feel funny. But anyway, they're laying us all off anyway at Christmas. They've got these new machines, they won't need us no more.

REG. 'Ope you're not falling into bad health.

CATHY. I'll be all right. I think it's me tonsils. There's something wrong with them actually, I don't know exactly. Once back home I had a job at the post office, and they told me I'd got to have me tonsils out, so I went along to the hospital, well they were very knife happy there at the time, there was a lot of them students, they said; 'Oh we've had a lot of your types through in the course of today', so then I heard screaming, one of them had wakened hadn't she? They had a coat to put on you and a thing to put over your mouth; I thought if they put that over my mouth I shall die, so then I ran out, straight out, never come back again.

REG. Tonsils is bad. We better get them seen to.

CATHY. It's not exactly tonsils, Reg . . .

The Anti-Natal Clinic

INSTRUCTRESS. Now, let's have another go at those exercises. Are you ready? Get into place. Right. Deep breathing. In. And in again. Now hold while I count ten. And slowly try once more.

At the Luxury Flat

The INSTRUCTRESS'S VOICE *continues describing the exercises as* CATHY *attempts to do them on her own. She doesn't do very well.*

Then we hear the voice of

CATHY. It came as quite a surprise when I found out. I was sick all the time and it never occurred to me why. So, the doctor he said, can it be that you're pregnant? And then I realised. I got to dreaming

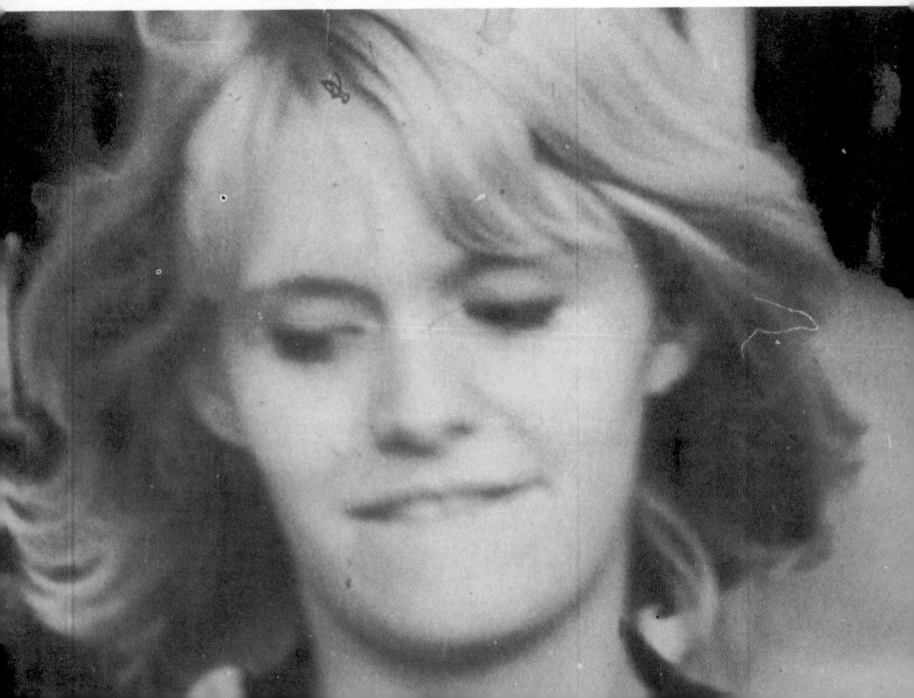

then, about what it would be like.

An Estate Agents Office.

CATHY. We're looking for a house to buy, can you help?

AGENT. We have a number of properties in the lower price ranges, £3,500 to £5,000, on which we could probably arrange a ninety per cent mortgage, all things being equal. May I ask how large your deposit would be?

CATHY. Well, I'm off work now, so we don't have quite so much just at the moment. But I reckon we might manage about £100.

AGENT. I'm afraid that means you're out of the running for a little time at least. £100 would barely cover the legal costs involved.

CATHY. But there must be some cheap houses that don't need too big a deposit?

AGENT. Well of course there are cheap houses, but these are invariably the older type of property, and a Building Society would not normally loan you more than seventy-five per cent of the price. That means for a £3,500 house, you would have to find £800, with legal fees on top of that, out of your own pocket. You might find a new flat with a deposit of £400, but you'd be very lucky. Of course if you were to move out of London, you might find you need no more than £250 as a deposit, plus your legal fees of course.

CATHY. Well, I suppose that's that then. From what some people said, I thought that it was easy for ordinary prople to own their own houses now.

AGENT. May I enquire how much your husband earns, as this will affect the size of the mortgage, should you subsequently be in a position to purchase a house.

CATHY. Oh, he earns a good wage–anything between twenty and twenty-five pounds a week.

AGENT. Unfortunately a Building Society won't take any notice of overtime, how much is your husband's basic wage?

CATHY. I think he's on fourteen pounds a week. It's not bad money you know.

AGENT. A Building Society will usually grant a mortgage of two and a half times the gross income On fourteen pounds a week, your husband's annual income is £728 a year, so that the maximum you could expect to be advanced would be £1,800, or thereabouts. To stand a chance of a house in London this means that you would have to find at least £1,500 from your own pocket. Even outside London you would have to find £700 or £800. You see we do have cheaper houses on our books, but they are in such bad condition that the Building Society would require you to spend £700 on improvements, and they would withhold a proportion of the loan until the work was complete. So really the cheapest houses are bought by people who have money in hand to improve them.

CATHY. So really it's a waste of time me coming.

AGENT. I'm afraid it is, yes.

A lorry gets into a skid, and crashes.
REG *jumps clear.*

REG *is carried off on a stretcher and we hear*

this conversation;

BOSS. What you mean, compensation?

REG. I need compensation.

BOSS. Free and easy. That's always been our motto, eh, Reg? Look Reg, you take the rough with the smooth. I ain't got compensation.

REG. I told you about that camshaft knocking though.

BOSS. Reggie, Reggie, look straight. Look, I'd compensate you Reg boy, but I'm skint. And I ain't had no insurance on me lorry. That's one lorry gone west, my friend.

REG. You're no friend of mine.

In Hospital

REG. Well, it's not very good, Cath. We won't have so much now. Never mind. Reg will fix it.

CATHY. How much will we have, Reg?

REG. You're not earning no more, and I'm down to sickness benefit. What's that, do you know?

CATHY. No. But not very much.

REG. How much we paying on H.P.?

CATHY. Ten pound a week

REG. Ten. And ten on the flat. Nothin' else?

CATHY. I don't think so. No. Oh, the Life Insurance.

REG. Oh yeah. Say twenty-two altogether. *Then he remembers.* But we got savings.

CATHY. Yes. About eighty pounds.

REG. Well we're alright then. I'll be back at work by then.

In Hospital (later)

DOCTOR. What is your profession, Mr. Ward?

REG. I'm a long distance driver.

DOCTOR. Quite a strenuous job I suppose.

REG. I'm afraid so.

DOCTOR. I've got rather bad news for you.

REG. I know.

DOCTOR. It'll be quite a long time.

REG. What d'you mean, quite a long time?

DOCTOR. Few months. Maybe for ever. That's as concerns driving.

In Hospital (later)

CATHY. S'pose we better be thinking about finding somewhere cheaper to live.

REG. S'pose so.

CATHY. Reg, we'd of had to go anyway cos they don't allow children there.

REG. Better go to Mum's for a while.

CATHY. There's no room is there? That's why Grandad had to go. The Council said it was statutory, overcrowding.

REG. They needn't know. She'll fit us in.

In Hospital (later)

CATHY. When the baby comes, will you be there? When it's actually being born?

REG. *Surprised.* I don't suppose so.

CATHY. Do be there.

REG. Why? What d'you mean?

CATHY. Well, it's your kid enit? You got a right to see it.

REG. *Doubtful.* I suppose so.

CATHY. Why should someone else be the first. Don't you want to be first to see it?

REG. I certainly do.

CATHY. Well then—

REG. Just, it seems a bit funny to be there.

CATHY. I think it seems a lot more funny *not* to be there.

REG. But can you do it?

CATHY. They say at the clinic you can now.

At a Flat-Letting Agency

CATHY *is talking to a* GIRL.

GIRL. Yes, flats for clients with children are very hard at the moment. Children are not popular with landlords, indeed they have not been since the war.

CATHY. So that shows in the price.

GIRL. Yes.

CATHY. What's the lowest price of a place for a couple like us and one child?

GIRL. In the sort of property we deal in, we don't have anything for less than six pounds. There are slum places at less but they're very shoddy. We don't deal in them.

CATHY. But that's an awful lot if you're not earning very much. My husband's been sick you see and we've only got about nine pound a week to live on these days and that's got to pay, you know, food and clothes and National Insurance and my husband's travel to work.

GIRL. So your husband is in work?

CATHY. Course 'e is. He's earning ten a week. He used to earn more but he had an accident. And, out of that we got commitments.

GIRL. So do you want the place at six pound ten a week?

CATHY. I'll have to ask my husband.

The Streets

CATHY *goes round doors knocking. She searches in newspapers, looking for a cheaper place to live.*

Meanwhile we hear the VOICE *of an* AUTHORITY *speaking on the housing crisis–how many houses and how many people to go in them.*

In the Luxury Flat

CATHY *is collapsed on a chair.*

CATHY. I think this is it Reg!

REG' D'you reckon?

CATHY. Yeah.

REG. Shall I ring for the hospital?

CATHY. *After a moment.* Yeah.

In the Ambulance

REG. Comfy?

CATHY. Yeah.

She clasps his hand to her breast as she lies.

REG. Don't worry. Reg'll fix it.

At the Hospital

CATHY *is wheeled out of ambulance.* REG *follows.*

In the Waiting Room or Passage

REG *is pacing about.*

NURSE ONE. *Sending him up.* From the state he's in I think he's having the baby.

NURSE TWO. Men should an all. They should have the first.

NURSE ONE. Why?

NURSE TWO. They'd be a little more thoughtful with what they do with women.

REG *doesn't register this. He is too worried.*

In the Luxury Flat

CATHY *and the* BABY. *We hear her voice;*

CATHY. I must have another one soon. I never knew it would be like that. Funny how a baby makes a place quite different. Well, there's goodbye to freedom. I don't mind though.

At Reg's Mum's Place

It is a flat in one of those high tenement blocks, built round a courtyard with interior iron staircases.

As we look around the area, we hear the VOICES *of some of the inhabitants describing it.*

VOICE. These are the only flats in the world where you can sit on the toilet and be cooking the dinner on the kitchen stove at the same time.

CATHY *is bathing the* BABY *in front of the fire. They're talking about the furniture they put in store.*

CATHY. No, let it go, let it go.

MRS. WARD. Ant you goin' to even put up a fight for it?

CATHY. Let it go. We can't afford to keep up with it can we?

MRS. WARD. I don't know.

We hear the VOICE *of;*

CATHY. Reg wasn't earning bad money. Just not what we were getting in the old days. The only thing was, Reggie seemed to get tired. His leg it was. Played him up so he found the work was tiring.

MUM. Then Reg's Uncle Mac, he was the adventurous type. He was out in India for a lot of his life. Wanted to see foreign parts he did, and he never married. Reg's Uncle Tom, he was in the Merchant Navy. Reg's Uncle Jim, he was the neer-do-well. I remember Granddad saying, when he got married, he said to him he did, he said, he's a nice man he is but he'll never be no use to you, or to no woman. Ever.

CATHY *is feeding the* BABY.

CATHY. Once there was a little baby whose name was Mylene . . .

At Reg's Mum's Place. Later.

REG, CATHY, REG'S SISTER *are eating.*

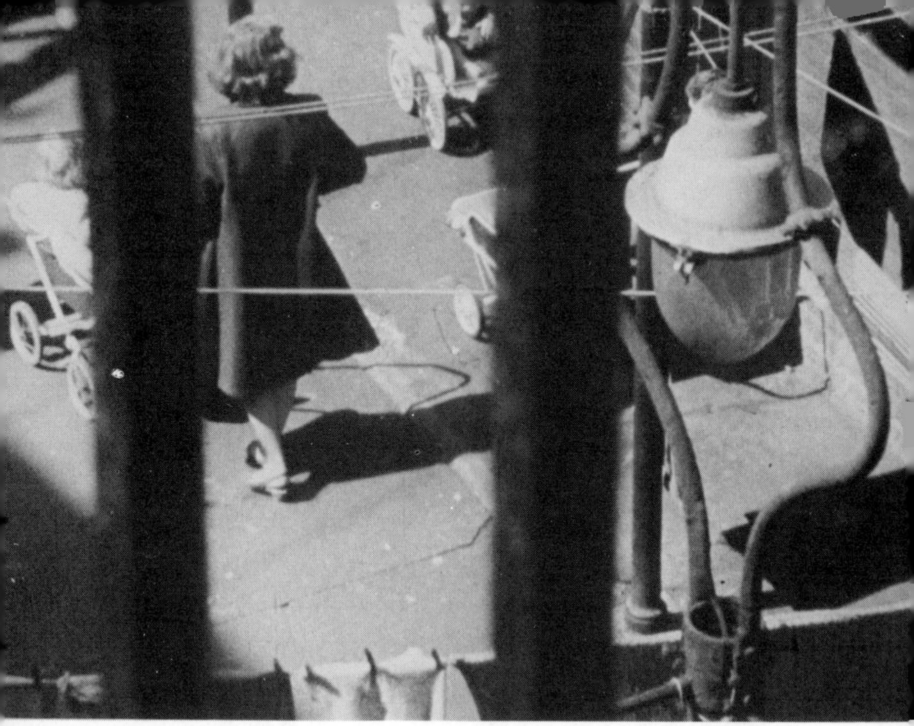

REG. Christine, do you remember that girl used to work at the bra counter, what was she, Christine Ramsbottom or something–

CHRISTINE. Oh, yes.

REG. Well, her boyfriend,–

CHRISTINE. He that used to be such a good runner at school?

REG. That's right. Well, he broke his leg. Has to have it amputated.

CATHY. He's not going to be much good at running no more . . .

They smile, then all laugh at her joke, although feeling that they shouldn't be laughing.

REG *notices something odd about the fish he's eating.*

REG. Hey, that's a funny sort of fish. Look, the most extraordinary fish.

EILEEN. Oh yeah. It's like one of them you got on those cigarette cards. Wait a minute.

From a drawer in the dresser she pulls out a set of cigarette cards with sea monsters drawn on to them.

EILEEN. Not that one. Not that one. Not that one. Maybe it's this one?

REG. They're none of 'em fish at all! No, but Cath, we use that place a lot. The *biggest* fish they have there, I tell you, this bloke does a deal of some sort, you wouldn't get a *live* fish for double the price you pay here.

REG'S MUM. Never leave. Why not. Never. Always live here like one happy family.

CATHY. What d'you think about them instant frosen chips? I give some to Reg Tuesday when you was out and he didn't think much of them.

MUM. Frozen chips! You know my views about them. You know what Mr. Ward says. More unhealthy. There's more sickness caused by them things.

MUM. You cook your dinner now dear, and then I'll cook ours for Eileen and the boys. No, you know it don't work when we all have it together, you cook yours now, and then, like I say, we'll have ours.

MUM. I'll clear up after the baby this time. I do think it's a bit hard the council won't do nothing for you. I mean, I've done my bit. I've brought up five children, I mean I'm not complaining.

Reg's Mum's. Seventeen months after the Wedding

CATHY *is bathing* BABY.

MRS. WARD *is sweeping. Dust going into the bathwater.*

CATHY. Look, be careful with that dust! It's all going into the water. Look, mind out!

MRS. WARD. You say mind out to me! In me own house! I'll teach you whose house this is, I will.

She violently resettles a chair which upsets soap and sponge CATHY *has been using.*

CATHY. Look, careful! How can I keep my baby clean?

MRS. WARD. Clean! You can't talk about clean. Look, how about that sauce what you poured down the cot? You ain't got much idea of hygiene. Stop your fella putting his feet all over the furniture. And picking up his child with his filthy hands.

CATHY. But he's your own son.

MRS. WARD. It was you taught him dirty habits.

CATHY. Dirty habits! You never wash your hands before you touch the baby or his bottle.

MRS. WARD. I was just helping you out. But you don't look after him.

CATHY. Right. And don't put Daz in his bottle.

MRS. WARD. Then there's the toilet.

CATHY. What about the sodding toilet?

MRS. WARD. You know what I mean about the toilet. I think it's disgusting.

CATHY. Well and to bring that up. Of all the meanest–

MRS. WARD. You got on my boy's nerves with worry, so he drove off the road. It's about time you was going.

CATHY. All right we'll go!

In the House in the Slum:
Three years after the Wedding

We are now in a different town and the house is reached down a narrow 'entry'. There are toilets in the middle of the yard that the back to back house looks on.

CATHY *now has* TWO CHILDREN–MYLENE *is two and* MARLON *is one.*

It is these kids that we see first. Perhaps they are messing around with a pigeon with a broken wing which keeps hopping backwards and forwards across the floor of the backyard, with them in pursuit.

Then one of the children falls and screams and CATHY *comes to rescue him.*

CATHY. Oh dear, oh dear, oh you poor little mite! You poor little fellow! Oh what a poor little fellow. Come on inside then.

We follow CATHY *into the little house.*

CATHY. Oh what a poor little fellow. Would he like a bok bok?

MARLON. Bok Bok.

CATHY. Bok Bok and bye byes.

MARLON. Bok Bok and bye byes.

Now the other kid begins to bawl, and CATHY *nurses it on her knee.*

We hear her voice in wildtrack;

CATHY. Reg and me we had a good deal of adventures and Reg had a good number of jobs and we went through a different succession of places to live and many times we was almost out on our ear and many times we was happy and our Marlon came to be a buttie for Mylene and now it was two years later, we moved right away out of the area where we'd been living and we found a place where, well, we reckoned it wasn't much but we could make a life, well, we had the kiddies now, and they give life to a place.

CATHY is chatting with a neighbour.

MRS. ALLEY. Ruby Dawn Alley is me proper name. I may have me funny ways, but I'm a kind-hearted old bit of sugar. I'm harmless. Just an old hag. What don't have nobody to turn to.

A conversation with ANOTHER NEIGHBOUR

MR. HODGE. It's about the toilet. Yup. I'm getting up a petition. Things have gone far enough. So they have in my opinion.

He holds out a grubby pad of notepaper.

CATHY. What's all this then?

MR. HODGE. Excuse me, missus, what I was tellin your husband this morning was worse than ever. The thing is there's too much pressure. Too many people! My word! I mean, the plaster's coming away from the wall, you go to pull the chain and great chunks of the ceiling come down, the chain pulls the ceiling down on top of you, so I mean it's slow, too slow. You're sitting in water all the time. Cistern takes half an hour to fill up! Half an hour! So with quite a sizeable concourse waiting, one can't follow the other!

CATHY. I'll sign your form.

MRS. ALLEY'S VOICE. Help! Help!

CATHY rushes into MRS. ALLEY'S.

MRS. ALLEY has fallen through the springs of her bed.

CATHY. Oh, Mrs. Alley, are you all right?

She pulls her out.

MRS. ALLEY. Oh thank you, ducks. Thank you. I really am grateful. Oh it's me own fault I know, me own fault, I wet the bed see, ain't I a naughty girl, eh? And the springs they got rotten. I go wee wee in me bed, the springs get rotted, it's me own fault see . . .

The Backyard

CATHY *is looking at* REGGIE*'s pigeons, holding* MARLON.

The voice of:

CATHY. Now I was pregnant again. Some would say it was wrong to have another kiddy when you're overcrowded as it is, but I don't think so. I think kiddies are God's gift; you don't do right to deprive anyone of the chance of life. Love's what's important in a child's life. Love is more important

to a child than what they call nice surroundings. I know cos I lived in what they call a respectable home and I didn't have it.

Montage Section

General shots of life in the area.

We see CATHY *and* REG *go past little gardens and bits of waste land.*

The voice of:

CATHY. I fell for it, all the parts round here, these streets, they looked rough, and there was rats but life was quite good here. Some of the places was boarded up, with the upstairs windows empty, others was stuffed, crammed full with people and kiddies. Once I heard sounds coming out from one of the boarded up houses, sounds of a baby crying.

At Mrs. Alley's

Afternoon tea, most genteel.

MRS. ALLEY. Now my dear, I once had a profession. Yes. Now guess what it was.

CATHY. I don't know. *She does.*

MRS. ALLEY. An 'ore dear, an 'ore! Didn't you know? Yes, once long ago, I was lovely. You mightn't think it. Had the fellas wild for me. And I was an 'ore.

She opens an old box or cardboard suitcase displaying just a few old bits of finery and a lot of letters.

Would you mind reading me this letter my dear? It's one of me favourites. I don't read so well now.

CATHY. Oh, Mrs. Alley, but it's all about sex!

A Back Garden

MR. HODGE *has a proliferation of boxes and cages, stretching through many stories and wings and annexes and turnings.*

MR. HODGE. Yes, this is a thing I feel very strongly about. I mean, we had a club and this club was about one hundred and fifty strong at one time, and well, now we've only got twenty members. I feel very strongly on that score. We were eight strong, we had children's parties with a couple of hundred kiddies, socials, dinners, functions and dances. We even took part in the Borough Victory Carnival. And now it seems that the British public have forgotten the good old British bunny. But in the last war I don't know where we should have been without him to help us along. The British bunny did 'is bit. The gallant British bunny he helped us with any number of succulent dishes—he did 'is bit—he helped production—he kept us goin'—he went to it.

He extracts a huge fluffy rabbit from its hutch.

MR. HODGE *continues.* Take the chinchilla, for instance. Now this is prized as a rabbit because it's got such a nice texture and such a lovely coat. Also it's more defined, now do you see, it has three different colours underneath the pelt, see? A base which is dark purple, then a nice purling which is as white as a pearl, and finally a black edging. Each hair on this rabbit, in other words, has three colours. The coat itself outside is, you might say, a mackerel top, which to my mind is something very nice to the eye of the female, especially if she has a coat, pair of gloves or suchlike made out of them. And now, if you would be willing, young lady, I would be pleased to donate you a mit that is made from these self-same pelts.

Outside Mrs. Alley's House

CATHY. I wanted to ask you a favour, Mrs. Alley. Could we owe you the rent a few weeks? The reason being, we're a bit behind-hand. What with the pigeons, and Reg, he don't earn very much now.

MRS. ALLEY. Owe the rent? Of course you can, dear. Mind I want to be paid. Want to be paid.

CATHY. We will pay.

MRS. ALLEY. I need the rent of you people coming in because old though I seem I'm not old enough to qualify for a pension, you see, I look older than I am and I find conditions very hard, now. But, yes, certainly, my dear, you can owe rent for a few weeks if it helps you.

In the Back Yard

They are waiting on the Sunday night for REG*'s pigeons to come back to the loft. And they are excited— the* CHILDREN *especially, looking up into the sky.*

REG. He has a ring round his leg, see, and when he

gets back into the loft you can take this ring off and it fits into a clock, and stops the clock, it's the only way of stopping the clock, and if yours is the first clock that's stopped, then you've won. Trouble is sometimes a pigeon sits on the roof or somewhere, he does, he won't come in . . .

They sit out on kitchen chairs in the crowded yard, and everyone all round is excited.

MYLENE. Pigeon! Pigeon!

CATHY. That's right—pigeon! Pigeon's not coming yet.

REG. He faces quite a lot of hazards along the way. There is the mountains, there is the sea, and there is that fellow they call the farmer with his shotgun, and then there is the 'awk. And they come from various distances, first down to Dover. Then from Paris, Marseilles. And then over the Pyrennean mountains, they chug down in the train to a little place or rather a fairly big place called Barcelona. And Barcelona, that is your one thousand mark. In getting to a place like this from a place like Barcelona the pigeon has got to go over the sea. Now, as he goes over and across the sea it so happens that the old bird gets vertigo. He gets afraid he may fall. *Romantically.* He sees his own shadow in the water you see, Cath. Then he swoops down, thinking that that is his shadow, and then as he goes on down, he goes on down and he never comes up again. No, he's gone see, he's gone down under the water.

MYLENE. Pigeon! Pigeon!

CATHY. No. Oh, look Reg!

A pigeon has appeared in the sky.

CATHY. Is it ours?

CHILDREN. Yes! Yes! Think so!

REG. No! Yes, it is!

The pigeon perches on the chimney.

REG *stands on one leg and the other, shouting in his anxiety:*

REG. Come along, come quickly, now come on, get into the bloody cage, get in, quickly, don't hang about, go in, go into the cage! Get in that bloody cage!

But the pigeon continues to perch, nonchalant, on the chimney.

REG. Quick, get in you bastard!

And slowly and coyly, its head on one side, the pigeon climbs down into the cage. The little door snaps to behind it.

We hear the voice of;

CATHY. I felt we was honoured, somehow, that pigeon coming all the way back from Barcelona to get back to us.

In the Backyard

Close up CATHY*'s running face.*

CATHY. She's dead! Mrs. Alley! She's dead!

At Mrs. Alley's

The great grey bulk of the old woman sits naked by the fireless grate, we see other pathetic details of the squalid room–gew-gaws, old newspapers, empty old suitcases, the window patched up with an old pair of corsets and some sellotape.

Meanwhile we hear VOICES;

FIRST VOICE: It was Mrs. Perkiss, she said to her, why don't you wash your clothes, they're lousy. That put her back up. Must of tooken em off then throwed em in the fire. And then she got so cold so she sat in the nude.

SECOND VOICE. They say it charred up her legs.

In the Backyard

The coffin comes out containing MRS. ALLEY, *carried by four men. We hear the voice of;*

CATHY. The men from the Council come along, took away her odd bits and pieces, they looked through the letters for notes of any relatives she might have but she hadn't got none, only letters from her old clients, that's all. So there was no one to pay the death grant to.

Outside the House in the Slum

CATHY *has opened the door to* CHIC, *middle-aged bureaucratic.*

CHIC. . . .A nephew of the deceased Mrs. Alley what died last week and the fact is, my client now needs the unpaid rent for the current week and the back period during which he gathers from the rent book that you was in arrears.

CATHY. I didn't know she had relatives.

CHIC. Well she does.

CATHY. Well, I'm sorry, but we can't oblige just at the moment. She did say we could owe for a while because Reg has been ill.

CHIC. What Mrs. Alley said and what my client wants are completely different. My client is your landlord now.

CATHY. Yeah but listen while I explain. While he's been ill we haven't actually been able to go on putting aside the weekly sum that we was meant to be putting aside for rent, because Mrs. Alley said that it didn't matter. Now he's better we'll pay up, of course, just give us a few weeks and I'll go out to work as well. We can pay double rent each week if you like.

CHIC. I don't want to know. I just don't want to know. Find some way to pay up.

CATHY. But–

CHIC. Find some way to pay up. You have been warned.

He walks off.

We hear the voice of;

CATHY. You couldn't talk to him. It was like it was hopeless trying to talk to him.

In the Slum House

REG *holds a letter in his hand.*

REG. Three months in arrears! I'll knock his block in! What's he talking about? How long since he come along?

CATHY. Three weeks.

REG. Three weeks! Well, they say here we owe for three months! Anyway, he never come to collect it. Who do we pay the rent to? Who are we expected to pay the rent to? He tells us he wants us to pay back the rent but then he can't even come to collect it!

CATHY. What does the letter say?

REG. Says we got to get out.

CATHY. It's nonsense. You can't be evicted these days. I saw. They passed a law.

REG. He seems to think that we can.

Outside the Slum House

CATHY. Look I've said if you'll only give us time, we'll pay. Look I know your game, you want to get us out so you can charge someone else for key money.

CHIC. My client needs this place for himself and his relatives. So you better get out. You may have heard that eviction is illegal these days. Well, in the case of a relative what wants the house, you can still be evicted. And we'll get a court order to prove it. We are in fact an old established agency. A man tried to cross us once. I fixed him. My client—

CATHY. Who is this client?

CHIC. Big. Big. He don't need to do his own barking. We do his barking for him. Look, even if it weren't for my client you'd soon be evicted sooner or later. Living in one room ent you? Well, the council have been evicting all you people. See, it's statutory overcrowding. Living in one room is now illegal. The Council got very hot on that.

CATHY. But, please—

CHIC. I don't want to know. I just don't want to know.

In Court

SOLICITOR for the LANDLORD. . . . Not only

persistently refused to pay their rent. In addition to this it seems, they have allowed the place to fall into such an extreme state of disrepair that the landlord will be forced to put the premises right at the cost of some hundreds of pounds to himself.

MAGISTRATE. What have you got to say?

REG. I'll say it's all a pack of lies. First, old Mrs. Alley said how she didn't want no rent because I was off of work, weren't I, and then when the fella comes along and says he wants the rent, but I went there with the rent and he wouldn't accept it.

MAGISTRATE. I am not satisfied in this case that Mr. Ward is telling the truth. In addition he appears to have 'waylaid' the rent book given him by Mrs. Alley. I take the case as proved and will grant an eviction order dated four weeks from now.

CATHY *is trailing around the streets with her kids searching for a place.*

CATHY. Excuse me, I saw a room advertised.

LANDLADY. That yours?

CATHY. Yes—there's me and three kids and my husband.

LANDLADY. Sorry, no children accepted.

The door shuts.

CATHY *continues to another door with a sign* Vacancies.

CATHY. I called about a room.

LANDLADY. Sorry. Sorry, no children or coloureds accepted. Or Irish.

As CATHY *continues to trudge in search of a room, we hear her voice;*

CATHY. So we tried, we wrote letters, wrote after places, never got no answer, and the next answer we got was, no children, no children accepted, and I went to an agent and he turned round and said, yes, they'd guarantee to find us a place, providing we gave then twenty per cent of a year's rent and ten per cent of fixtures and fittings, which I thought was unjust. And I wrote letters and the rent was too high, there was one place we did go to and I thought we were going to have a chance, they said six pounds, and the next thing we heard someone offered them eight, so that put the cap on that, and other letters we got, ten pounds a week. Because Reg couldn't afford it, not on his wages, it meant that all the week we'd be living on next to nothing.

Outside Another House

ANOTHER LANDLADY. Yes dear, I think we could fit yourself in. Don't have no kids I suppose?

CATHY. Well, I have got three.

LANDLADY. Sorry, no children.

CATHY *continues her search, peering among the notice boards.*

We hear CATHY*'s voice;*

CATHY. It wasn't long before I realised something. We'd been lucky to get the old place. There didn't seem to be anything for us any more.

And we hear another VOICE *say;*

VOICE. I see they're putting a car park for thousands of cars on Clapham Common. Well why can't they put houses there? They put houses there in the war. Do they think that cars is more important than people?

The Street

Again CATHY *is trudging down the street.*

CATHY. Everywhere it was 'no children, no children'. If I'd of had a couple of elephants they might of said: 'Fair enough, you can leave them outside in the yard'. But children, they'd say, 'Sorry, we can't have nothing like that.' It was as if they thought it was a crime to *have* children.

In a Cafe

MYLENE. Mum, why do people have babies? Is it cos otherwise the world would run out of people?

CATHY. No, it's because they love them.

Outside an Apartment Block

LANDLORD. Yes, I've no objection to children, but it will cost you money. Now, can you put down £100? If you can, then you can have the place. Are you willing?

CATHY. It isn't a case of being willing, it's just we haven't got it.

At the Town Hall

CATHY, *the* CHILDREN, *and* TOWN HALL OFFICIAL.

CATHY. So can't you put us on the housing list?

OFFICIAL. Listen, in this town we have about eight thousand units whose housing need is very grave. That's about one out of every twenty units. They're people who are gravely over crowded. Perhaps, in extreme cases, teenage brothers and sister may have to share the same bed. Perhaps, it is a crippled person living on a top floor who thus can never go out. They may be sharing with relatives. They may even, like you, be under an order of eviction. To house these eight thousand units we have about five hundred new dwellings every year. So that the average family is about sixteen years on the list. People's needs are assessed by points. One point for health risk, one point for every year you've been in the borough, one point if you have no bath. Now you don't really qualify with enough points: but in view of the gravity of the situation I will investigate whether we can't arrange for you to jump the queue a little. In view of the situation I'll try to see that you get a place on the new Smithsonian Estate, just nearing completion.

In the Slum House

CATHY *sits with her* CHILDREN.

THE OTHER CHILDREN *are looking at the* BABY.

MYLENE. No, cos they're fat, and they small, an all the time they go, wa, wa, wa.

CATHY. Oh, poor little fellow. Wait till he's a bit bigger then he'll be able to do all your jobs for you, like go on errands for you and that.

THE CHILDREN *continue to play with the* BABY *and we hear the voice of;*

MR. HODGE. Well, I wish someone would do something for us, re replacement housing. Yes, I do think if they put their minds to it they could do more for us than they are doing. There's plenty of waste ground in Britain as one can see by travelling on the buses, where they could do a lot more, build flats or houses, whichever they prefer, and give us all a front door, let us live happy. But they don't do it.

REG *sitting with the 'Pigeon Fanciers Journal', takes it easy on an old box or broken chair.*

REG. Listen. We're not going. Nor you. We're going to refuse. We got to be firm.

MR. HODGE. I told him that. But, look, he used bad language. He insulted me old woman.

REG. Listen, don't go. I'll look after ya.

MR. HODGE. We'll have to go. Cos they told us.

At the Slum House

A MAN *stands at the door with a briefcase. We hear* CATHY*'s voice;*

CATHY. One day we had a visit from a man from the Council, told us we was overcrowded. Although we had two rooms the second one was too small to count as a room as far as he was concerned. We'd have to leave.

She says to the MAN;

CATHY. But listen, we're going to be evicted anyway.

HEALTH INSPECTOR. Oh, really? Is that so? Really? When's that then?

REG. Next Tuesday.

HEALTH INSPECTOR. In that case, I'm spared having

to do something which personally I don't believe in.

He goes.

REG. Faceless man, ent 'e? Faceless man! Why don't he do something about it, 'stead of just doing things he don't believe in!

At the Slum House

A MAN *stands at the door with a briefcase.*

We hear the voice of;

CATHY. So then it got almost like a madhouse, things split on the stairs, the washing pulled down from the line, the lights pulled out from their sockets, even windows taken from their frames in some of the houses. Someone turned off the water and the wires for the electric got all pulled out.

By a River Bank

There are boats moored by the river, drawn up on the mud, crazy collections of old rotten hulks, some once noble steam yachts which have been converted and others, caravan bodies that have been placed on rafts made of kerosene cans.

REG *had been wracking his brains and he remembered this place.*

CARETAKER. Yes, we used to have people living here but now we can't allow it. The thing is, families deteriorate when they're living in a boat. We used to have them, but it was a slum. If people want to

come here with their pleasure boats and take them out occasionally, that's all right by us. But to live in them the whole time, in my opinion, it doesn't help anybody. We had to ask them to go.

REG. But what if they're homeless? That is they've nowhere else to go?

CARETAKER. Even so. It's not helping them. In my opinion, we had to turn them out. It's not helping them to help themselves.

At the Slum House

REG *puts corrugated iron across the inside of the windows and the doors.*

Meanwhile, we hear the voice of;

MR. JACKSON. Now in this Odyssey, that we have been witnessing, of course we have been hearing the story very much from the tenant's point of view. But you know, there is another side. Our side. I'm speaking by the way with authority from Jackson and Jackson, the holding company in this case responsible for the property in question. Now I know it's quite common for the police to be brought in for an eviction. There's nothing unusual about that. But it does get people's back up. It's bad publicity for the company that owns the place, particularly in respect of the fact that that is in fact a reputable body of churchmen who, purely through the application of good business methods, have landed themselves in the unfortunate position of *seeming* to do an injustice.

A BAILIFF *approaches with a heavy sledge hammer. At a nod from one of the* OTHERS, *he begins to bash at the door. The door begins to move.*

REG *has piled all the furniture against the door. Now as the door begins to give, he goes and adds his own weight to the furniture.*

Finally, the door is forced.

REG. That's it, Cath.

REG *and* CATHY'S *furniture is brought out and dumped in the street.*

A shifty-looking MAN *approaches* REG.

MAN. Tell you what, want me to store your furniture, Mister? Want me to store your furniture? One pound a week?

REG. Get away will you?

A MAN *is putting a padlock on the door.*

REG *runs at him head down, butts him in the stomach, but* CATHY *restrains him.*

On the Way to the Caravan Site

A refuse dump and a canal beside it. Beyond the canal black mountains of cinders. Three TEENAGE BOYS *roaming this territory in jeans and boots, with guns. Strange birds hop about.*

Now we see REG *who pushes a collapsible pram piled high with their belongings, suitcase, etc. And*

MYLENE, MARLON, *followed by* CATHY *with* MAVIS *in her arms.*

It's a cold evening with a touch of rain. The CHILDREN *are whining a little.*

MYLENE. How long till we get there? Mum? How long till we get there? 'Cos I'm squashed, *flat!*

CATHY. I told you. Nearly there, five minutes, Reg?

REG. *Hopeful, but without conviction.* Five minutes? Oh, yeah, should be there any minute now. Want to change again?

They are proceeding along an apparently endless concrete causeway flanked with wire mesh.

Two horses grazing beside the causeway. Two lorries jacked up on old pieces of wood.

MYLENE. Mum, how long we going to be now?

CATHY. Look, Dad told you, any minute. And don't spoil it now that we're nearly there!

MYLENE. Where we goin' to live now, Mum?

CATHY. You'll see.

The Caravan Site

Backed by a wood, there stand here two gaudy Gypsy caravans, one battered roadmender's shelter square on its tall wheels, many other caravans, and a converted single-decker bus.

CATHY. Which one is it, Reg?

REG. Over there.

CHILDREN'S FACES *peer out at them as they pass, then disappear again.*

They reach a caravan and REG *tugs to get the door open and they climb inside.*

Inside the Caravan

CATHY. Is there any light?

REG. Wait just a minute. It shall be showed you.

CATHY. There you are love then. This is where Marlon's going to live now.

MARLON. We going to live in this caravan? Where we going then? Are we on holiday?

REG. That's right, we're on holiday;

MYLENE. We're not going anywhere silly. This is the sort of caravan you stay still in.

REG. Now, easy does it.

REG *has lit the Tilly. Then it goes out.*

He lights calor gas, puts the kettle on, fusses about.

CATHY *changing the* BABY'S *nappy, putting it to bed.*

We hear her voice;

CATHY. It wasn't too bad finally. The wind was

getting up outside, in the marsh. It made it feel quite snug inside. It felt funny to be in a caravan. I'd only been once before and that was in the summer on holiday. It was a relief though really. I think it was cos of the tension we'd been living under in the past few weeks.

In the Caravan. Later.

CATHY. Hey! But Reg! What about the bed? There's only one bed! We can't all get in that!

REG. Panic! Panic! Keep calm! It shall be showed you.

He tugs at the bed which is the sort that folds right up against the wall. It comes down.

They lie down together on it. Smile. They've come through.

In the Caravan. Later.

CATHY *fiddles with a button on* REG's *jacket.*

CATHY. Are you sure we're safe here? You sure we can't be moved from here? They won't come and get us?

REG. Here? Look for us here? We're safe, here; nobody cares about us here. Not with this lot. We may have dropped a peg Cath, but we'll be a lot contenter.

We hear the voice of;

CATHY. Later the wind got stronger. It began to rock the place around quite a lot. . . .

The Caravan Site. Next Morning.

We hear 'Housewife's Choice' on the radio as we see the encampment as it wakes up.

We see MEN *with high cheekbones and long uncombed filthy colpons of dark hair dressing.* WOMEN *lighting fires.*

Washing hanging beneath the trees.

CHILDREN *peering out from recesses under vans.*

GIRLS *that are pale and sullen.*

The TWO BEAUTIES *of the encampment. One, blonde wears pinks and purples, and stockings with a lot of holes in them. The* OTHER *is browned-haired and more solid. They are washing themselves in a cauldron they've placed on a tree stump.*

The woods that the vans stand on the edge of must once have been beautiful. Now they are filled with filth, rags, broken glass.

There is still a trace of mist among the trees.

CATHY *makes up her face.*

The Caravan Site.

CATHY *is talking to* MRS PENFOLD.

MRS PENFOLD. Never. Never. I see no air in a 'ouse. An' I don't think a 'ouse would suit me. I see no air and I like the air because air is life and my life is beautiful because you know we're rough and ready but we do love it. Because I'm eighty-six.

CATHY. Eighty-six!

MRS PENFOLD. Eighty-six and I don't think a 'ouse would suit me. In a van you're right in the air. Well, in a 'ouse, there's all brick walls round you, you've got no air in 'em. And I don't think the life would suit me, a 'ouse would suit me, one to sleep, let alone one for living in.

The Caravan Site. Later.

REG *and* ELI BRAZIL.

ELI BRAZIL. Yes, well, some of the vans here is fine made. Mine is a fine made caravan, it costs so many hundreds of pounds and it's decent. It's decent. And, as I say it's got the heating. It's very warm, very dry, well, you know, often times it's raining in Britain, there's no rain come through here nowhere. No winter air nor draughts. Just lined with fibre glass. I've got it warm. I've got fire heating as good as a 'ouse, in many ways, in my opinion a van is better than a 'ouse. What would you say? Cos you're from the houses.

Now we see them sitting round a fire, CATHY, CHILDREN, MRS BRAZIL, ELI BRAZIL.

ELI BRAZIL *has a bronzed face, brilliant white teeth and wears a viridian and ultra-marine hanky knotted round his neck, which sets off his purplish eyes.*

CATHY. Well, yes, I was, till the other day.

ELI. There now! So how d'you like it? How do you like the open air life?

CATHY. I didn't think I was going to like it really. But now, well I haven't had time yet really to tell.

ELI. Happy folk. All of us. Happy. Better happy nor dwellers in houses. You'll see. All happy. Now, you like to see inside the van? You kiddies? Like to see in the van?

MYLENE. Yes!

CATHY. Well say it politer than that. Say 'Yes please, Mr. . . .'

CHILDREN. Yes please Mr. . . .

Inside Eli Brazil's Van

CATHY, CHILDREN, ELI BRAZIL, MRS BRAZIL.

It is piping hot from the little iron range in the corner with its chimney that goes up through the roof and the whole thing is polished, scrubbed, glittering and gleaming, all cut glass and maple wood.

ELI. Yes, cost so many hundred of pounds, and its decent as you see. The interior as you see is all light maple, there's three separate rooms–

MRS. BRAZIL. *Two* rooms, Eli.

ELI. There's *three* separate rooms, and the upholstery as yer see is all light pink leathering, in fact, we've got everything we could need.

MRS. BRAZIL. Of course it ain't always been like this, because when you get old you can't do what you want to do, can you, 'specially when you get our age. We travelled round the country, years ago, we never stopped at one place long, see, we was on the road, travelling. Used to love it, we were all healthy and well. Beautiful life, happy, everything was lovely that time of day, there was a lot of difference today. Better food, we worked hard in the fields, and we done a lot of travelling around, all round the country. We never stopped at one place very long. We were on the move again. And now we are here stationed, and it's not the life we used to have. Such nice times. In them days long ago we had twelve ponies, two horses, two lions and several small animals, and a couple of bears. Unfortunately when the big shows came out on the road, well, it didn't really pay because we were playing off the beaten track, sort of, and the expenses, they were too great, and we had to pack up. And now we are here stationed, and the only thing is, it's not the life we used to have. Not such nice times.

ELI. Yes, sometimes, you know, you do long to be

back on the road. 'Specially when the sun comes out. That's what makes us feel unsettled, you know, here comes the nice weather and you know that you've got to stay in one place, cos the country, I mean to say, Devon and Cornwall and Somerset, the country is lovely travelling you know, 'cos you meet such beautiful people, changes of face, change of country, you know, real lovely. When we're tenting we do practically a different place every day, see, we're practically in a different town every day, and it means pulling down at night, and going on the road, and when the summer time comes it's just lovely.

The Jones's Caravan

CATHY *and* REG *are sitting in a run-down caravan, the home of despair. Only two bunks in it, no sheets, and blankets that are rimed and filthy with black grease.*

MR. TALMADGE, *a man with a huge red unshaven face, asleep.*

MRS. JONES *and* FIVE CHILDREN *sitting round. Opened tins on the table.* MRS. JONES *making much of the newest* BABY, *perhaps because it's not had time to get dirty yet. There is no fire in the stove. A vast black dog climbs over them.*

MR. JONES *nods his agreement as she talks.*

MRS. JONES. It's the housing you see. When Mr. Jones came out the forces he went trying hard to get places, but the money he got wasn't good. As the children came it got worse. He went down the mines, he went as drivers in buses, but each time the rent we was asked was too much. Too much for his wages. He tried for jobs on the forestry, which each time we have been turned down. He's willing to try he'll do anything. He's a real sticker. He just don't get that chance. He did forestry when he was a prisoner of war. But we just don't seem to get the chance . . .

In the Caravan

MYLENE. Tell us a story, Mum.

CATHY. Which one?

MYLENE. You know, the bedtime story.

CATHY. O.K.

They snuggle up beside her.

CATHY. Once upon a time there were three children, their names were Mylene, Marlon and Mavis, they lived in a magic castle.

By an Open Fire

REG *with* MR. ALEXANDER.

MR. ALEXANDER. There's a lot these days will say, oh he's just a dirty Gypsy! But we ain't dirty. We're clean. We keep ourselves clean. We wash ourselves. We don't need their flush baths. Our way is, we get a bucket of water, we wash ourselves down, say down to our waists. And then we wash down that part, pull our shirts down, take off our trousers, and then we wash ourselves down and up, up and down, down and up, up to the bottom. And you'll never find no fleas nor lice nor louse, because we know how to thwart them. The devil's dung. The devil's dung, well, he has a sort of stink . . . it could be staggers, it could be cholic, it could be bugs and louse and it don't matter. We thwart em. That's with the deveil's dung what we get off the chemists. And when folk see a Gypsy they say 'Oh don't he stink!' But we don't stink. And this smell they smell on a Gypsy is nature's gift.

CATHY. Marlon, what's wrong with you then? Are you all right? No, you're not all right. What's wrong?
Marlon is sitting very frightened.

In the Caravan

MARLON. Mum. How big can a little fish grow?

CATHY. What size of fish, love?

MARLON. Well, a tiny fish. This long. Could it grow to be a great big forty foot monster?

CATHY. Oh no I don't think so.

MARLON. You sure, Mum?

CATHY. Yes. It couldn't grow that big, why do you ask?

MARLON. 'Cos Ruby said, there's a little fish got into the puddle down the road, and Ruby says it might come out and attack us, when it got great big.

CATHY. No, it couldn't do that, love.

CATHY *hugs him.*

MARLON. Well, why did she say it?

CATHY. I expect she was trying to tease you.

MARLON *goes out to join the* OTHER CHILDREN *again.*

At the Caravan Site

We see the daily life on the site, the changing of calor gas cylinders, chopping wood, getting water.

Meanwhile we hear the voice of;

CATHY. Reg got a job picking black currants and when the job with the black currants was over, he got more work at the airport, on the new runway, and then, picking gooseberries. And the kids liked the life here, they wandered round in the Shillington woods with the other children, it was quite a good playground really, they were for always finding things that fascinated them among the trees. I got to like it here, Dunno why. It was squalid, but it was easy goin, only sometimes the filth got on your nerves. I worried, shouldn't Mylene be going to school. But they said no. The local school wouldn't even have her. So for the moment we was all right. I felt as if we'd sunk somehow out of the race. Things didn't seem to matter down here no more. There was no one to move us on. Reg and me reckoned we might stay here a while. It was a life. We was happy.

The Church Hall of the New Estate

The RATEPAYERS *are holding a meeting.*

Women's Institute Banners, a cross, etc., are ranged round the hall.

DEMBLEBY. What we are pressing for is the fencing off of the common land so that Gypsies and layabouts can no longer get on it. Now it is the traditional camping place of the Gypsies, of course, no one is denying that. But these are not real Gypsies. Scroungers. Layabouts. These are the sort of words that spring to one's mind on contemplating these people. And of course, with the new housing development of which we are all part, the character of the area must be expected to change. We're living in a new modern Britain. We can accept no hindrance from those who wilfully try to keep us in the past, there is no longer room for slums on wheels in modern Britain. They will be better off elsewhere.

Murmers of agreement.

This is a high class housing development. And, between you and me, consider the possible effect on resale prices.

FROUDE. *Diffident.* Of course I do in fact believe that many of them are not in fact Gypsies. They are there in fact because of grave housing conditions.

DEMBLEBY. Grave—now let me tell you this. If nothing is done soon there will be a roar of anger from our residents. There has been talk on this estate of action being taken against the Gypsies. One can only smooth things over for so long. Trucks and caravans have been parked 100 feet from our houses. We have to keep our windows shut because of smoke from the fires.

CLOUGH. *Crafty.* Where would the sympathies of the Association lie in the advent of violence breaking out between members of the Association and the Gypsies?

DEMBLEBY. In the event of violence breaking out between ourselves and the Gypsies, sympathy must be shown to one side or the other. And in this event I am afraid our sympathies will be very much with ourselves.

VOICE. This council has wasted enough time on these Gypsies. They give nothing towards this council so why should we support them?

SECOND VOICE. I have had the unfortunate experience of having these people on my boundary. My neighbour was kind enough to pull down the trees, thus leaving the site exposed to the four winds.

THIRD VOICE. I sometimes think I am fortunate not

to have been born one of these people. They have to live. They are people like you and me. Surely we should cater for people who cannot look after themselves as well as for those who can.

FIRST VOICE. Yes, but young respectable couples in this borough cannot now get housing loans. Who would we rather have the money?

At the Haywain Pub

A notice says: 'No Gypsies served'.

REG, MR. *and* MRS. JONES, TALMADGE, *and MR.* ABERCANDER *are having a drink.*

MR. ABERCANDER. . . . collecting the scrap up, keeping it tidy, all the old scrap what the council throwed away, old tins, bicycle frames, beadsteads, old rungs, old metals, in that line of business, and then when I weren't doing that, this was the period of pickin' cherry and apple. And again, of a later year, also hog tradin', potato picking up, sugar beatin', mangos. And so it happened that, in a ditch, I came on Mrs. Abercander . . .

REG. Was she in the ditch as well?

MR. ABERCANDER. Yes, well, we'd both had a bit too much.

PAULINE JONES, *Mr. Jones's daughter breaks through and comes running through the pub;*

PAULINE. Mum . . . Mum . . .

She stands frantic, a touch of lipstick round her fourteen-year-old lips.

The Caravan Site. Night

The JONES*'s caravan is on fire, a terrible blaze.*

PEOPLE *including* CATHY *standing about, trying to run into the blaze to rescue the* CHILDREN.

OTHERS *ineffectually throw water.*

Meanwhile we hear the VOICE *of the;*

CORONER. Why were you living there in the first place?

MR. JONES. We was evicted from the Council house in Stoke.

CORONER. Where were you on the night of the fire?

MR. JONES. We went out to buy some dolls for the kiddies. Then we stopped for a quick one.

CORONER. Did you and your wife have to be out together to 'buy dolls for the kiddies'? Or 'have a quick one?'

MR. JONES. Mrs. Jones can't drive. I wanted her advice about the dollies. And there are times when a man and his wife have to go out together, and this was one of them. And I would say, Sir, that this was murder. The children from the new estate, well the adults there they just encourage them.

CORONER. Yes yes yes.

Later

CORONER. Now Miss Pauline Jones, were you asleep in the caravan on the night on April 25th?

PAULINE. Yes. We was all six in the bed. I woke up cos the place was full of smoke. So I took Garry in

me arms and got out.

CORONER. And then?

PAULINE. Well all the others got burnt up.

Later

CORONER. Now, you are the Health Inspector for this region. Would you agree that pigs are better housed than these people?

HEALTH INSPECTOR. It is a matter of housing.

CORONER. It is idle to tell me it is a matter of housing when you yourself have made orders for the demolition of houses a thousand times better than these caravans.

HEALTH INSPECTOR. The local authority have full sympathy for these people.

CORONER. How have you shown sympathy? These caravanners have been living under foul conditions, and not willingly.

Later

CORONER. Mrs. Jones, will you confirm that there was a previous fire in your caravan, on June 2nd 1961?

MRS. JONES. Yes.

CORONER. What was the reason for this? Was it caused by a candle falling over?

MRS. JONES. I can't remember.

CORONER. Try to remember, Mrs. Jones.

MRS. JONES. I can't remember, Sir, it was some years.

CORONER. We are concerned with the death of four

children.

MRS. JONES. *Shouts.* Will this bring four kids back? Will it bring back my kiddies?

The Caravan Site.

The caravans are being moved by dust-carts, tractors, lorries.

There is a smell of wood-smoke, and dogs and horses gathered round. Down the concrete causeway comes a further procession of tractors and lorries. Some of the drivers look embarrassed. The police look sullen.

Meanwhile a MAN *in a tweed jacket and old school tie goes round from caravan to caravan, asking them to move. The lorry drivers hitch up the caravans and wagons and begin to tow them away.*

One by one the caravans are hauled out of the wood, and away down the concrete causeway. They are towed to the verge of a nearby clearway, and there dumped.

That night, a new collection of lorries and tractors make their appearance, hitch them up, and again transport them away, some of them to a common, and others to other laybyes.

Meanwhile we hear the VOICE *of;*

MR. JONES. Oh yes, it was quite unusual there. That was a very unusual place cos the bloke that owned it liked us. Generally it's, well, like it is now. They push us on the go all the time, push and shove all the time. Oh yes. They send a squad car along and they come and see how many's there, and they count them, and then they just take out summonses, you see. Then they get the cans and they tow them over the boundary to where the jurisdiction of the next lot begins. And then they leave you aside of the road and they summons you for being aside the road. The reason being that we can't have no obstructions beside the public highway.

In the Caravan

They are sitting down to dinner in the caravan where it is parked by a laybye.

REG *about to light the Tilley lamp.*

MARLON. Please don't Dad. Please don't light it. 'Cos we can sit in the darkness! Please don't light it so there's a fire.

REG. It's all right, Marlon, really, Dad's clever with the lamp, he won't let the place catch fire, like the other place did.

On the Road

We see the caravan being moved on and dumped, moved on and dumped, and hear the VOICE *of;*

CATHY. Reg was still trying to go out to work and what with all this dumpin' and movin' on and then again dumpin', Reg got to the state he didn't think much of it. He never knew if he went out if the van will still be there when he gets back. He was working at the airport, but some nights when he comes back, he couldn't find us, the van's been moved, he had to ask all round, you seen my van? Then he was late for his bit of food, then he was tired in the morning Or maybe he couldn't find us, he had to sleep rough and then go to work the next morning, and he'd be worried about us, so he got behind in his working.

In the Caravan

REG. We can't go on like this. I'll sell the Caravan. I got offered a twenty-five for it. We'll try a different town. There must be somewhere for us.

A Derelict Street in a City
A few days later

A bulldozer starts to knock down a wall. REG *runs up.*

REG. Hey! What you think you're doing mate? You're not going to knock it down? Look, I just rented two rooms in this house!

BULLDOZER DRIVER. You're in for a draughty evening mate.

An Abandoned Car. Early Morning

REG, CATHY, *and the* CHILDREN, *are all in an American car abandoned in a narrow alley.* REG *is shaving out of a teacup, looking at his reflection in the car mirror.*

CHILDREN *still asleep beneath blankets on the seats.*

REG. Yes, well that's fine, I reckon. I reckon when my Dad married her, she must of been attractive.

CATHY. Mmm, mmm, could be.

The Abandoned Car. Later

HEALTH INSPECTOR. I am required by law to investigate occupied premises to ascertain whether in fact or not there might be a health risk. Ah. Got the kiddies here too, I see.

REG. Listen. We're going. We're just going. We've got a place. We've got a place to go today. Look, say you haven't seen us.

HEALTH INSPECTOR *looks at him over the top of his glasses.*

HEALTH INSPECTOR. I am a fairly tolerant kind-hearted fellow.

REG. Please. Don't get us arrested and have the kiddies taken away. That don't help nobody.

HEALTH INSPECTOR. I tell you what. I'll forget that I've called for one day. I'll come back tomorrow. Provided you're gone by then I'll be prepared to have a mental lapse about today. But make sure you're gone. I was sent here. That means somebody knows about you.

A Derelict Building

A few nights later.

CATHY *washing clothes which she hangs on a bit of string hung across the room.*

REG *putting bannisters and boards on the fire on which*

they're boiling water.

There is no light in this place other than candlelight and the plaster has come away from the wall.

The KIDS *are playing with* TWO OTHER THREADBARE KIDDIES.

A YOUNG GIRL, *filthy, enters*

CATHY. Do you live here too, then?

GIRL. Yeah, me and my kiddies. Till they turn us out.

CATHY. Is there many living like this then?

GIRL. Quite a number in these roads, round these parts. Your little girl don't look very well.

There comes a heavy hammering on a distant door.

In a Derelict Part of Town

REG *and* ANOTHER MAN *walking along a street.*

MAN. Why are you doing it? Can't find a place?

REG. Don't seem to be able to find nothing.

MAN. *shakes his head.* You people let yourselves get so run down. No wonder they won't have you.

REG. We get run down because we aint got houses. It's no good, this life we've been leading. I wonder sometimes when it'll end.

MAN. We've got a Welfare State now. You can't come to real harm. Are you an inhabitant of this borough actually? Are you on the housing list?

REG. Yes.

MAN. Whereabouts on the list are you? Surely you must be pretty high?

REG. Well, they did promise us a place on the Smithson Estate, when it's completed.

MAN. The Smithson Estate! You're laughing! The Smithson Estate is nearly completed! Be done within three months or so!

A Barn filled with Hay Bales
A few days later

REG *is attempting to construct a shelter from bales.*

MYLENE *is now not well at all. There is a wind blowing and the tent whisks away once more out of* REG*'s hands. There are splashes of rain coming down on them.*

As REG *begins once more,* CATHY *puts her arm on his shoulder, draws him slightly away from the* CHILDREN.

CATHY. Mylene's not well, Reg. Reg, I don't know what you think, but I think we've had it actually. They turned us out of the motor and out the cellar didn't they. Well I suppose they'll find us here as well. Soon, I think we'll have to give up soon. Else they'll take the kiddies away like he said.

REG. All right. I know, honey. I've got five pounds left.

In a Cafe in a Park

REG, CATHY *and* CHILDREN *eating.*

REG. So, you know where you're going tomorrow?

CATHY. Mm. Pity about that place at Shrewsbury.

REG *is not sure if she does know, they've never discussed it.*

REG. Yes, but, you do know where you're going?

CATHY. I know.

In Cumbermere Lodge Home for the Homeless

They are in a large bare room and TWO OFFICIALS *sit opposite her across a small table.*

CATHY *is just finishing signing a form that begins: 'I hereby apply . . .'*

OFFICIAL. Now Mrs. Ward, you say you have an Aunt in Northumberland?

CATHY. Yeah, well yeah, I did have.

OFFICIAL. But you don't know her address?

CATHY. I aint seen her since I was seven. She might be dead as far as I know.

The MAN *makes a note.*

OFFICIAL. Other relatives?

CATHY. No. Look, I told you—I come from a foster home, didn't I? And they don't want to know.

OFFICIAL. Now Mrs. Ward, have you any *friends* or any other relatives anywhere in Britain that might help with offers of accommodation?

CATHY. If I had I wouldn't be here.

OFFICIAL. I am required to draw your attention to a fact, which, well, it's not very pleasant. In our emergency accommodation– it's not very nice. And some of the inmates, well, they're a little rough. Now are you sure you want to go in?

CATHY. Look, I don't want to be cheeky, but we've already been six hours here. Do you think we'd of stayed if we had any choice?

OFFICIAL. All right. Sit down. Mr. Ward, please.

CATHY *returns to the* CHILDREN *who sit on benches.*

REG *gets up and sits by the table.*

OFFICIAL. I'd like to check certain facts with you, please, Mr. Ward. Now, you and your wife were living with your mother till what date exactly?

REG. January '64.

OFFICIAL. At what address would that be Mr. Ward?

REG. 197 Maysoul Road.

OFFICIAL. Really? Really?

He thinks he's detected REG *in a lie. But, no it's just that he can't read his own writing.*

OFFICIAL. Not Mayberry?

REG. No, Maysoul.

OFFICIAL. Oh, now. Other relatives. Um, your wife's mother? Where does your wife's mother live?

The Same. Later

OFFICIAL. Do you have any sisters?

REG. No.

OFFICIAL. Oh. I thought, Mr. Ward . . .

REG. Except me teenage sister. She don't count. She ent got a house. She's still courting, ent she?

OFFICIAL. Grandmother or grandfather?

REG. Grandfather. I have got a grandfather. But he's in a home.

OFFICIAL. Now, Mr. Ward, how many rooms does your mother occupy? That is, at May–soul Road?

REG. There's a lot of rooms but there's an awful lot of them.

OFFICIAL. How–many?

REG. There's two on the top floor, then underneath, two rooms, and underneath that two more, and the back kitchen. But there's twelve of them living there already.

The Same. Later

OFFICIAL. The accommodation we have available is for wives only, we can't accommodate husbands.

REG. Why can't husbands be accommodated?

OFFICIAL. We used to house husbands at one time but we had to discontinue the practice. They used to tear up the sheets.

The Same. Later

CATHY *and* REG *sit in front of him.*

OFFICIAL. We've got no objection to your coming to see your wife on a weekday evening. That is provided that you are gone by eight.

The front must not be used by you homeless. Again there's a good reason. It does upset the old people we also accommodate here–and of course this accommodation really was meant for them.

Now. No alcohol in the building, This is one that we are fairly strict about. And we do expect inmates to take a regular bath and get plenty of fresh air.

CATHY *and* REG *look at each other.*

OFFICIAL. Rent. We charge five shillings a night for each adult and three bob for a child. Payable in advance.

REG. What, do we have to pay rent?

OFFICIAL. We can't put you up for free, let alone feed you. Right. Any questions? There are other rules, but you'll find it easy to pick them up as you go along. Now any questions?

REG. Well, I don't think much of it.

OFFICIAL. In lots of places in Britain they don't keep families together. They break them up straight away when they become homeless, put the children in care, etc. etc. The Welfare Department of this city, in their wisdom . . .

REG. Can't you give us a flat? Can't you? So we can stay together?

OFFICIAL. The average family on our waiting list has to wait years for a house. If we re-housed homeless families, then everyone would see it's an easy way to queue barge. No, we can't do that for obvious reasons. And it must strictly be understood that this is only temporary. After three months, make no mistake, we turn you out. So keep searching. Right. Sit down.

The Same. Later

REG. Don't worry.

CATHY. I'm not worried.

REG. Look, love, it won't be for long. We'll find some way.

CATHY. We'll be all right, I know. Pity about that place had to be demolished.

REG *looks at her for a moment, with love for her in his eyes.*

Time passes. The CHILDREN *are hungry.* REG *gives them some chocolate.*

CATHY *goes up to the desk to ask how much longer will they be, and the* MAN *behind it gestures her back. When not interviewing people, he's talking into a telephone.*

The OFFICIAL *looks up;*

OFFICIAL. Mrs. Ward!

CATHY *gets up and goes over to him. He writes something on a piece of paper which he hands to her.*

You'll be in room E.72. E.72. Don't forget it.

A Quadrangle of Cumberland Lodge

They are walking to CATHY*'s room.*

NURSE. Hey, you, get out, shoo!

REG. I'll just take her up to her room.

CATHY. We've only just come.

NURSE. Oh, you're new, are you? No men beyond the lodge. Not at this time of night.

MAN. I'm sorry, but you'll have to say goodbye to your wife now.

REG *makes to go.* CATHY *turns after him.*

MAN. No, not you, girl.

REG. Can't I stay with her? She's– she's–

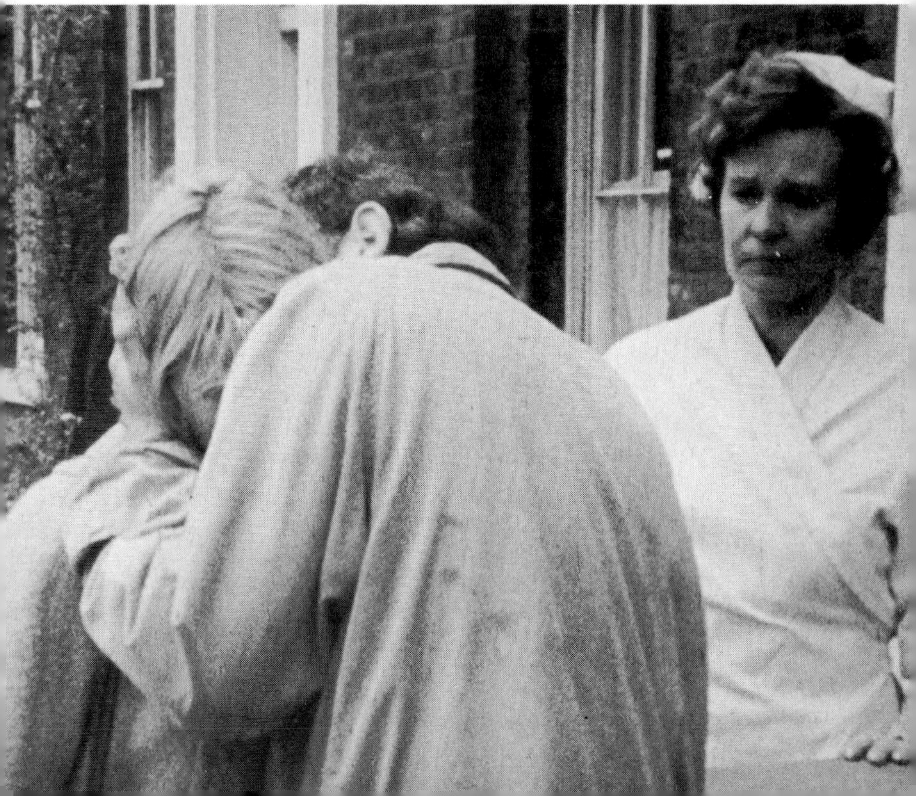

CATHY. If he could stay with me, I'd–

MAN. No, no. Sorry. I didn't make the rules.

NURSE. Now, get out, shoo! She's got a lot to get through yet.

REG. Now, steady on lady. Don't you try to be saucy with me!

CATHY. Reg, don't.

REG. Goodbye.

REG *and* CATHY *kiss goodbye.* REG *turns away and walks off. He looks back once.*

MAN. You go that way.

CATHY *and the* THREE CHILDREN *cross the quad.*

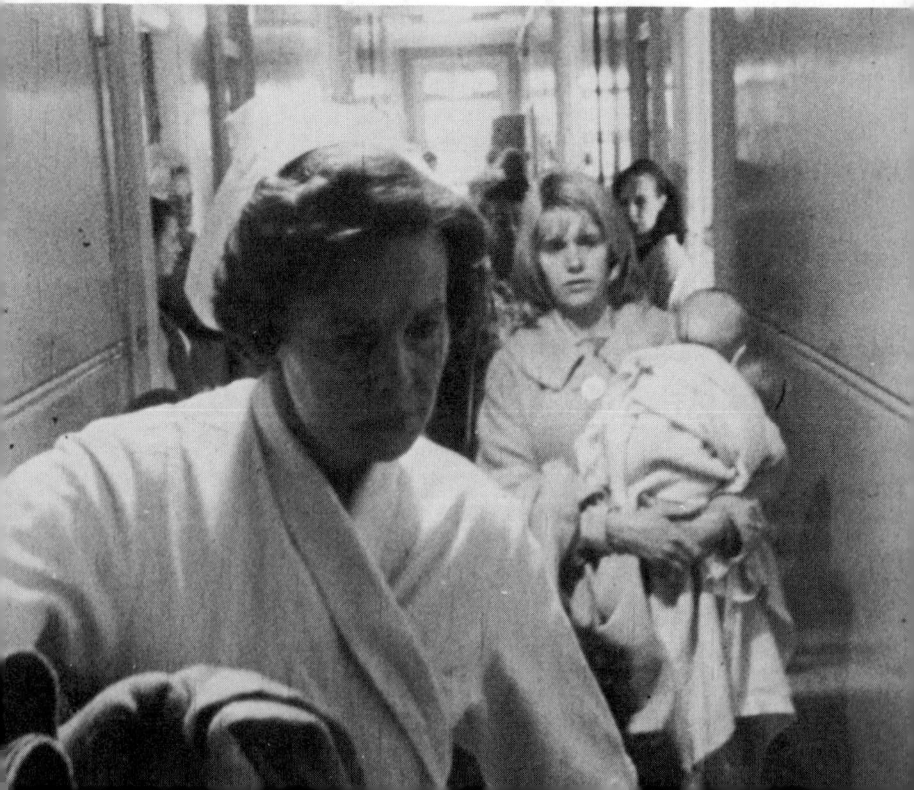

The Blanket Store

CATHY *and* WOMAN *in a room filled with blankets and sheets.* WOMAN *giving some to* CATHY. *One of them is bloodstained, as if someone had coughed blood over it and some of the blood had remained although it's been washed.*

WOMAN. Here you are. By the way, watch it here. Keep your children clean. There's disease here.

CATHY. *Not aggressive.* Why do they send us here if there's disease?

WOMAN Oh, there's disease in all these places.

The Swabbing Room

CATHY *and* CHILDREN *have preliminary swabbing.*

CATHY. What you have to do is take down your panties. That's right, and then they're going to put something up your botty. It won't hurt you'll see, it won't hurt.

MARLON. But why do they want to do it?

We hear the VOICE *of;*

CATHY. Mylene always was the worst at taking down her pants, she never wanted anyone to see her without them.

The Dining Room

CATHY *and* KIDS *have cups of tea in a vast empty dining-room.*

CATHY *traverses corridors. Past doors through which she can see glimpses of* OTHER FAMILIES. *Stone pillars, and a notice flapping against one wall:*

UNDERSTAND

That all children and persons that live in PART III Accommodation . . .

They walk on. Passages branch away on either side. There are narrow passage-like rooms in which WOMEN *are washing at basins in rows.*

And everywhere, ragged and not so ragged CHILDREN. WOMEN *standing around heavy with child.*

The place weighs down on CATHY*'s spirits. She is thinking 'Is this what we've come to?'*

For the top floor there is no light. The stairs are concrete, flanked by iron pillars.

In Cathy's Room

CATHY *finds the room with E.72 scribbled on a piece of paper stuck to the door with sellotape.*

There are two beds, with blankets made up into military squares. Hanging on the wall, we see the 'Rules'.

CATHY *puts the* KIDS *on one, and starts to make the other. She puts the* THREE KIDS *on the made bed and herself gets into the other. She's lonely.*

In Cathy's Room. Later

CATHY *in bed. Then we see the door open and a figure outlined against it.*

REG. *Hoarse whisper.* Cath!

CATHY. Reg!

REG *makes his way across to her bed.*

CATHY. Reg, what you doin here?

REG. I climbed in. Met another husband just outside showed me a way over the wall. I couldn't leave you alone, love.

CATHY. How did you know where to come?

REG. I remembered the number.

CATHY. Shhh!

She hugs him.

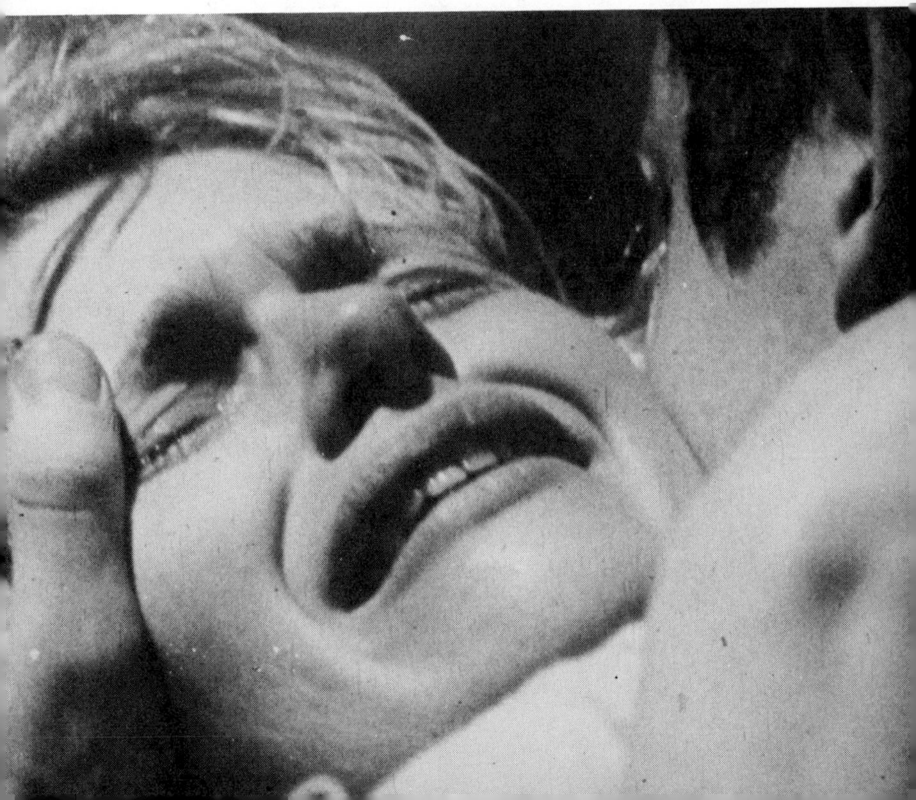

CATHY. Oh I'm glad you've come, Reg.

The Same. Later

CATHY. But what about the morning?

REG. I'll go betimes. Have to anyway. Got to get some work.

They embrace and make love like they used to in their early love-making in the room down Mantua Street.

CATHY *cries.*

The Dining Hall

As they queue for breakfast, MRS. MURPHY *squashes up to them.*

MRS. MURPHY. Here ye are then. Here's a fine lad! Oh and isn't he a fine one! Oh, and a lovely boy, and isn't he a fine one!

MARLON *moves back against* CATHY. CATHY *stands back herself.*

A CHILD *catapults against her, knocking her back against* MRS. DARKE.

CATHY. Oh, I'm sorry.

MRS. DARKE. Sorry! *Is it sorry?*

CATHY *takes her tea and plates of bacon and bread from the servery, she goes and sits with the* KIDS *at one of the long tables.*

MRS. MURPHY. And we've been here full three years now.

CATHY. Three years!

MRS. DARKE. You never. Not all here, three years.

MRS. MURPHY. First at Briarwood. Then at Newton House. Then Holm Lea. Now back here. Ha. Some places is better than this. Hm.

MRS. DARKE. There, see. She's not been here three years.

CATHY. But did you never have any hope of getting away?

MRS. MUPHY. Oh yes, yes, yes, yes. There was plenty of hope. Hey!

Her eyes fixed on the cup in CATHY*'s hand.*

MRS. MURPHY. Hey!

CATHY. What's wrong?

MRS. MURPHY. Never do that dear. Get another cup.

CATHY. What d'you mean?

MRS. MURPHY. Look. Keep away from the cracked mugs. There's sickness in 'em.

Another table. MRS. TOVY *and* MRS. CONOD.

MRS. TOVY. And they'll send you back.

MRS. CONOD. Send us back? To where?

MRS. TOVY. To where you're from. They'll send you back. But not before. Oh no, no.

MRS. TOVY *breaks into tumultuous coughing and spitting.*

MRS. CONOD. But to Somerset? They'll never send us back there then?

MRS. TOVY*'s cough turns to a laugh.*

MRS. TOVY. Oh, they'll send you back and all. Yes, they'll send you back.

MRS. DARKE. Yes, and why don't they send *you* back then? You don't belong in this country, why don't they send *you* back?

MRS. TOVY. And do I not belong in this country? As well as yourself?

The WOMEN *seem they are going to have a fight.*

MRS. DARKE. Mr. Keene will–

MRS. TOVY. Ach, who's afraid of Mr. Keane.

MRS. DARKE. Mr. Keane will–you wait now, Mrs. Tovy. Mr. Keane will explain to you and no questions. Mr. Keane will make it clear.

MRS. TOVY. Eh?

MRS. DARKE. Mr. Keane will explain it to you!

MRS. TOVY. Eh?

MRS. DARKE. Get back home you *foreigner*!

MRS. DARKE *strikes* MRS. TOVY. MRS. TOVY *is complaining querulously to herself.*

MRS. TOVY. Get back home. Och did you hear her, did you hear the lady then, och did you ever hear the like.

The Washroom

Various WOMEN *scrubbing* CHILDREN.

A smartly dressed WOMAN *leans across and says to* CATHY *in an affected voice;*

MRS. GABY. Drop in for a drink some evening.

CATHY. Oh. Thank you.

MRS. GABY. F.20. Some of the people here are low. I can see you belong to a better type of class. When my husband and I first arrived here we thought we had come to the end of the world. We came by taxi actually—so much luggage—well most of these people one feels that their belongings would fit in a carrier bag, but we had some decent trunks, you know. We arrived in this place, and all these women were crowding round, fingering our luggage.

CATHY*'s life seems to become more disjointed and people and places don't seem so clear to her now.*

Squared between low twin-storey terraced houses, we see behind her Cumbermere Lodge like an old-fashioned fairytale, there are tall Victorian style gateposts and on their top cracked gas lanterns and another in the centre. And beyond, a black carriage drive stretching steeply upward, winding through unkempt grass, winding up to the tall grey beautiful building, standing up against the sky, pinnacled and turreted and battlemented in profusion, like a castle from a fairy tale, window after window, it must be eighty windows along the front.

The doors in the centre of the facade have long steps leading up to them, where CHILDREN *play. Some of the noble windows are cracked. They have curtains up half their height or none. Old newspapers blow up from the asphalt and out of the central doors, from which also erupt* CHILDREN.

Cumbermere Lodge

We see scenes from everyday life in Cumbermere Lodge; CATHY *and the* KIDS *play in* CATHY*'s room.*

Scrubbing the corridors CATHY *is called down to the Warden's Office.*

A LADY *has brought in concealed alcohol.*

Washing nappies and sheets.

Families trying to hang curtains over the curtainless windows.

Calling in KIDS *off the roof.*

Meanwhile we hear the VOICES *of various* INMATES.

INMATE. They don't want to make it too nice.

Otherwise they say they'd have us here for ever.

INMATE. I was in the council house weren't I? So then me husband pissed off, and they have a scheme there, that if you're an abandoned woman they turn you out they do and so then I come here. They say it's to stop men leaving their wives. But it didn't work in this case.

INMATE. We were living in a rented house in Margate and it was needed by the Works Department for a road widening scheme. So we got an eviction order and they said they couldn't rehouse us because they were not the welfare authority and they didn't have any houses.

INMATE. We put our furniture into store at a pound a week, and on the day the bailiffs were expected it was a day of terrible snow and he came and we had to be out by eleven and I said it's only ten-thirty and he said we can't evict you on a day like this into the snow, but as soon as the snow is gone we'll be back to evict you. So we stayed on in that house without furniture for another week, and my husband stayed off work to be with us. And when the snow finished the bailiff came back to evict us.

INMATE. We went to the Welfare man at twelve and he said you can't come now, I'm going to have my dinner. And so we went out and came back at two-thirty and he kept us waiting till three and then he had the cheek to ask if the babies had been born out of wedlock.

INMATE. He said, go to the station and we'll pay your fare. We travelled on the train, and we got out there, where they said, and they told us, you should have gone on further. So we waited half an hour and got the next train. And the station master said, I'll ring up for transport, but don't go thinking you can take your pram, unless you want to push it. So I said I'll push it. And I did. I walked those two miles pushing it. We arrived here and there wasn't even a fire in the grate.

INMATE. Scrubbing, scrubbing, that's all it is all day here. We have to scrub the place out twice a day. You'll see.

INMATE. We said, can't we have a radio? So the matron she said, what, and all have different programmes? It'd be babel!

INMATE. The children is the ones that feels it the most. They miss their toys, the little things they've had since they were tiny kiddies.

INMATE. We were payin' seven pound a week and my wages were eight pound a week. So I mean, it was hard, it was hard . . .

The Visiting Room

REG. I try to figure it out. I don't understand. We had money once didn't we? And earning good money. And then I lost the job when I had the accident. And then I sold the van to pay the down-payment on the house that was demolished. and each time we lost on the deal, that's what I don't understand, and now here we are at the bottom, but we wasn't always, that's what I don't understand. And as time passses we seem to be sinking lower.

CATHY. We'll be up again. We're down now but we'll be up.

REG. Oh yes, we'll be up again, no question. Reg'll fix it. But it's funny, I used to be all right on me own, on me tod. But it's funny. Once I got used to you, and to having kids, I didn't seem to feel that way no more about nothing. You get to need the wife and kids, like, to tick over. And now I don't seem to be able to tick over on me own. It just don't seem to be the same thing, it don't seem to tick.

CATHY. The Warden, he said, if there's a repeat of the incident what occurred last night, he said, if there's a repeat, out you go. So of course I denied it. I said I don't know what you're talking about. So he said, I have my information.

REG. Pity.

At Reg's Mum's

CATHY. Mrs. Ward, I wanted to ask a favour of you.

MRS. WARD. Oh yeah.

CATHY. I've come to a decision about Mylene. I've decided it's not fair on her to let her stay in this place where we are now. She's pining I can see that. So what I wondered is, could I leave her a few days with you?

MRS. WARD. Leave her here? What d'you mean? You can't walk out on your children like that, what d'you mean? Leave Mylene with me? You must be out of your bleeding mind.

CATHY. You don't understand, I don't want to leave her, really, it really gets me, I wouldn't let her go, only I can't stand it to see her taking it bad, I can't bear to watch it and think of her being in a place like that, and I can't stand to see it.

The Same. Later

CATHY. Goodbye Mylene. Be good.

The Visiting Room

CATHY. You act like you was uneasy. Sit down.

REG. I am uneasy.

CATHY. Sit down then. Then you won't feel so uneasy.

REG. I'm sorry. I feel I'm in prison here.

CATHY. What about me? I have to live here.

REG *picks up* CHILD, *plays with it.*

CATHY. Reg, I don't like to ask you, but Mavis needs shoes now very bad.

REG. Listen Cath, I'm only getting ten pound a week myself now, ent I. And I'm giving you six. That leaves me with four. Fifteen bob goes on me National Insurance, and one a week on the furniture what's in store.

CATHY. Yes,well that leaves three pound five.

REG. Well, the lodgings are two pound ten. That leaves five bob a week for me clothes and me food. How d'you think I eat and clothe meself on five bob a week?

CATHY. What meals do you get in your lodgings?

REG. Worse luck. Just me breakfast.

CATHY. How do you manage then?

REG. I'm starving. I was going to ask, couldn't you do on less?

CATHY. We couldn't possibly, Reg.

REG. How much is the rent here?

CATHY. Five bob a day for a grown up and three bob a day for a child. That's three pound three a week, without Mylene.

REG. Well, what's the rest going on?

CATHY. Oh Reg, don't be like that. You have to get out of this place. We spend it on food.

REG. Don't they feed you here?

CATHY. There's disease here. I can't let them eat there. One day was enough.

REG. You better had.

CATHY. Why?

REG. They'll starve else.

CATHY. Yeah, but they'll get diseased.

The Same. Later

REG. I did think we'd got help, Cathy. A bloke told me someone might be able to help us, and I went along to see this fellow and he started making the forms out saying 'Where are you living now?' And I told him, I'd moved into this kiphouse, and he said, 'Oh well, then I really am sorry, the thing is I can only help people who are resident in this borough.'

The Same. Later

REG *puts his head in his hands and says;*

REG. I've failed you Cathy.

The Washroom

MRS. MURPHY *turns on the taps of the basin, and begins to scrape at her arms with the scrubbing brush.*

A stream of blackened water comes from her arms and hands, she is being very thorough about it, entering into it heart and soul, peering from behind her pebble spectacles at the jet of dirty water.

CATHY *is just getting down to giving* MARLON *a little wash when suddenly who should come in but* MRS. KEANE *at a great pace. As she comes in she is shouting;*

MRS. KEENE. Ach again! Ach again!

She points a plump arm at MRS. MURPHY.

MRS. MURPHY. Ah tis you again, tis yourself Mrs. Keane, tis you again, tis yourself Mrs. Keane, ah fockett.

She returns unperturbed to her washing.

CATHY. What did you want?

MRS. KEANE. Didn't they tell you that was my basin? Didn't they? Didn't they?

MRS. MURPHY. Ah, fockett.

She snaps off tap, the plumbing gives a jerk, dries her face with her hands, then goes to lavatory.

Ha–ha–do you hear me? See where it's written?

MRS. MURPHY *points to a piece of dirty paper with a pencil scrawl over it, tied to the back of the basin.*

She returns with paper and begins to crackle it over her face.

MRS. MURPHY. She sees your bit of paper.

Stretching out her hand she tears it off, throws it down on the floor and stamps on it.

MRS. KEANE. *shouting.* Ach, did you so? Ach, did you *so*? Ach, Mr. Keane will see to that. Mr. Keane will see to that.

MRS. MURPHY. *spitting, shouting.* Go now, you horrible woman!

MRS. KEANE. And did you hear her? Did you hear her? Washing your hands at my basin in the washroom!

MRS. MURPHY. The washroom she tells us—

MRS. KEANE. My basin.

MRS. MURPHY. What's it to you?

MRS. KEANE. What's it to me? I'll tell you what it is to me, I'm a law abiding citizen, I'm not going to stand by—

MRS. MURPHY. You what?

After a brief pause, MRS. KEANE *says matter-of-factly;*

MRS. KEANE. I'll get the warden.

MRS. MURPHY. You do that.

MRS. KEANE *strides matter-of-factly to the door, then turns;*

MRS. KEANE. Ach, you lecherous Irish bastard.

This jibe really does seem to upset MRS. MURPHY.

MRS. MURPHY. Well, I'm not that, I mean I'm not that I'm not that, I can prove it. I'm not a bastard. I can prove it. Well, am I? Do I look like a bastard.

The Quad of Cumbermere Lodge

MATRON. No, she's got it. I'm sorry, she'll have to go. You can come with her as far as the hospital, but the other child can't.

CATHY. What shall I do with him then?

MATRON. Leave him in the grounds. He'll be all right for a couple of hours.

CATHY. Can I telephone my husband?

MATRON. There's no phone dear, you know that. He'll be all right.

CATHY. I don't like to do it.

The Same. Later

MARLON *hitting his head against a wall.*

In a Hall at Cumbermere Lodge

BENSON. Now, Catherine Ward, you've been here three months, as you know this is the maximum period that we allow homeless families to remain in our temporary accommodation. Now, the first thing I think we'd all like to know is, have you found a place of your own yet?

CATHY. Well . . . I have been trying.

BENSON. How?

CATHY. Me and Reg've been looking on the notice boards. And we went to the agents. But we don't never seem to have no luck. We wouldn't be here if there was a chance.

BENSON. You see, we've been housing you without statutory obligation and without legal responsibility to do so. The idea was to give you a breathing space in which to make your own arrangements. As a result of people like you we are severely restricted in the number of beds we are able to offer to the elderly and the insane.

CATHY. I understand all that.

WARDEN. This is only temporary accommodation, you see, we do in fact have the power to evict you. We could very easily say, Well that's enough of that, so much for her. As they still do in many towns in Britain. We could turn you out and take your children into care just like that.

CATHY. Please don't.

WARDEN. But we're not going to. Instead, we're going to give you one more chance. But I must emphasise to you that this is your last chance. You must make your own arrangements. We've made arrangements for you to go to what we call Part III Accommodation. This, like the place here, is one of our accommodations where the husband is not admitted. You're not going to like it there—the amenities aren't anything like as good as in this place, but, it's the best we can do.

CATHY. But don't you think, the thing is sir, couldn't you find somewhere, some sort of place where I could get my husband back with me?

WARDEN. Some families here have really been trying to get back on their feet.

CATHY. Who d'you mean? And how? I've not met any. It's not possible, not from this place. They can smell that you're from this place. They can smell it a mile off.

A CLERK. Now, don't be saucy young lady.

CATHY. I'm sorry. Something's happening like—I don't exactly know how to put it in words, this, it's having a bad influence on my family life. I did hear say that you had some places they call 'Halfway House' where the husband can be there too. And if I got to Halfway, I might be able to persuade Reg to come back, cos I feel well, it's not for me so much—I feel he's drifting away and the kids need him. I wish you could put us in Halfway House. The other thing is it would only be for a month. Because after that we got a place.

BENSON. You've got a place in one month's time?

CATHY. If it's finished. Yeah. We're going to the Smithson Estate. They're giving us a flat there.

BENSON. We've checked on your claim. We are told that you lost your place on the list long ago, owing to moving. Five hundred families have already moved in.

CATHY. But we was meant to be one of them families.

The CLERK *whispers a word in* BENSON*'s ear.* CATHY *shouts at them;*

CATHY. Runts! I saw you laughing there. Wipe that smile off your face! Aint you got room in your houses? Aint you got one single room? Or aint you got offices, empty half the night I shouldn't wonder. Runts! You don't care really do you? You only pretend to care. Oh Gawd. I shouldn't have shouted at you. I didn't mean it. I'm sorry.

As if nothing had happened, pleasantly;

All right, Mrs. Ward, that will be all for now then.

Exit CATHY.

MRS. GREEN. Well, what's your opinion, warden?

WARDEN. She's not an easy person by a long chalk. Keeps her children quite tidy but—well, as you see, she's not too co-operative. In my opinion the trouble rests with the other half.

BENSON *and* OTHERS. Oh, really. Really.

MRS. GREEN. Nowhere you could put her, I suppose, *with* Mr. Ward?

CLERK. Nowhere.

BENSON. No, absolutely nowhere. We're full up as it is. Mr. Firbank will tell you. We've reached the state that if there were two more families come in tonight, we'd have to evict from here to make room for them.

The Big Room

A big room filled with beds, subdivided by screens, like a stable.

WOMEN *and* CHILDREN *scattered round their beds, talking quietly.*

One GIRL *is lying weeping on her bed.*

The OTHERS *ignore her.*

CATHY *has just entered with* MARLON *and* MAVIS.

CATHY. Hey–don't cry–don't cry–what's happened?

INMATE TWO. Don't heed her. You can't help her.

CATHY. Why's she crying?

INMATE TWO. She got the letter.

CATHY. What letter?

INMATE TWO. The letter that evicts you. They just come now and took her kids away. Be all right on her own.

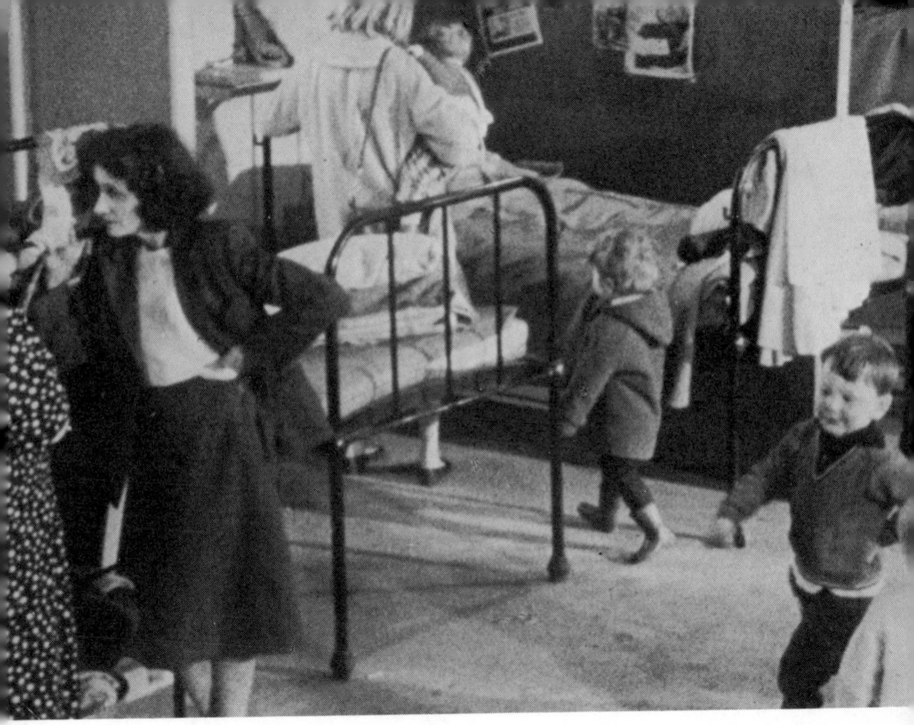

The INMATE *looks up for a moment and we see that she is the girl* CATHY *saw once before in the derelict buildings.*

Light comes from dim bulbs. Beds stretch right across to the further walls, and there are radiators contained within silver-mesh grilles, and a warm fetid stench and under some of the blankets great hulks of WOMEN *and* CHILDREN *already sleeping.*

CATHY. This is where Marlon lives now.

CATHY *settles* KIDS *into the same bed, one top, one bottom.*

INMATE THREE. You the one never went to see your little baby when he was in hospital?

CATHY. What d'you mean? I went every time I could didn't I?

INMATE THREE. Not what I heard.

CATHY. I couldn't visit her every day. It was too far. I 'adn't got the money for my fare. And I wouldn't leave my other one.

INMATE THREE. I used to walk when my kid was in hospital.

CATHY. I couldn't leave my other one. And when I went, and the little one cried, I couldn't bear to see it.

Holm Lea

We see WOMEN *dressing and undressing their* KIDS.

*Communal kitchens–*WOMEN *jostling round stoves.*

CATHY. How long do we stay here then?

INMATE. Seven years.

CATHY. *Appalled.* Seven years!

Sitting on the beds around her, the OTHER WOMEN *begin to talk in a sort of dirge;*

INMATE. Seven years I put up with this sort of thing; seven years I been here.

CATHY. Seven years!

INMATE. Turned us out, didn't they? Turned us out in the street.

INMATE. When I come here they said, Who told you to come here? I said no one told me, did they? I grew up here.

INMATE. My man, I was in the army six years. He was a regular, wasn't he? Well, that don't seem to count.

INMATE. The trouble is my husband. He was using filthy language. They won't let them come outside at the weekends you see and he give them the side of his tongue. They don't seem to like us after that.

INMATE. I'll give you a tip, dear; don't go taking a bath. 'Cos there's tramps what sleep there.

INMATE. And the toilets get blocked.

INMATE. And you can't see them now, but there's cockroaches here behind the plumbing. Comes out at night. One inch long.

INMATE. I was bombed out in Plymouth. Then I was two year in a mental home. Well, I'm not to blame for that, am I?

This is a squat angular WOMAN *wearing gym vest, dirty square navy blue skirt, and old plimsolls.*

INMATE. 'E's got a fancy girl now. I hate 'im. Men don't have it like women. He's free.

INMATE. In the war we used to dream of the good old times we'd have when we got peace. But Britain's not the place it's cracked up to be.

INMATE. People outside say that we was refugees. When we went to the baths they said they didn't want refugees in their baths and their first thought, wherever we go, seemed to be that we was refugees. I went round the welfare and they said, Oh, you're a refugee.

INMATE. I first come in the reception, they told me, leave me gear 'cos I wouldn't want it, they told me, bring in the clothes I was wearing and for the kiddies. So I left all the saucepans. I left cheese grater, I left bedroom suite. I left nutcrackers. I left cocktail cabinet . . . and I left all the toys for the kiddies. So, she was using 'em, I said no, but she said, I won't, but she did, and then she was very distant these days, there was talk about me, a lot of cheek if you ask me, old cow and that, well, it's God's will I said, to have that number and besides that, it was only natural.

INMATE. You feel ashamed. If you're walking along the road back from the pub and there's other people going parallel to you, and then you have to turn in here.

INMATE. Mr. Perkins let on he'd got a wife and kiddies on this place. Well, that was the end. No job. You see, they say as we're feckless.

INMATE. So they hired us all out Tellies. We just give the street number, they didn't realise that we was here. Then they found out. They come to get 'em all back with a van and a couple of policemen.

INMATE. There was this peeping Tom used to come round. He painted black crosses on the doors. One day we all got together and chased him up to the roof. But we never caught him. There was some said it was the warden.

INMATE. I went in front of the committee, they said, why not put your two oldest in institutions. Then we can rehouse you, they said. So I said, give me that in writing. But they said, that's not the way we do things.

INMATE. Everybody round there considered that we were either unmarried mothers or girls from Borstal under corrective training. But that wasn't so.

INMATE. People–they won't give you credit for anything if you wish it, and, well, people call you refugees which isn't fun. I mean . . . I went round the welfare and they said, Oh, you're a refugee. Well being from this town, you know, all your life, and all your family come from these parts, you felt embarrassed as well as angry . . . they think you don't pay your way and you're living on charity, and they don't realise the housing is as bad as it is.

INMATE. Last June it was I lost him. The disease, it was. He was only ten weeks old, poor little creature.

INMATE. The husbands go off, that's the trouble. They get fed up not being able to sleep with their wives or have their shirts ironed or even a bit of food cooked up for them. My husband says, this rate and he'll be back inside again, he was inside once, before I met him, but this rate he never sees us and he says it's enough to drive anyone to it.

INMATE. They say, go out and get looking for houses. But we know it's a nonsense to go out looking for houses.

INMATE. When we first came here the Warden said we could only stay for a couple of days, but we've been here six years.

INMATE. I got a fifteen year old boy out and they wouldn't let him come in. He was walking the streets at night and nobody could do anything for him.

INMATE. When I was walkin' on Tuesday, I saw a row of houses they said had been empty for years. They were big houses, could of got twenty or thirty families living there altogether. And I said Who's the landlord? And they said, The Queen. Well, I don't believe that. I don't believe the Queen would keep her houses empty at a time like this.

The Same. Later

CATHY. D'you ever think of leaving him?

INMATE. Yes, I did think of it, but what's the use? I think it's silly, when a girl gets married, thinking a bloke is going to be faithful to you, for instance, my friend Mary's like that, she's so certain. Proclaiming to everyone. But I still maintain that I'm better off married to Len than what I would be without him. If you love a person, there's not much point in leaving him. That's right. That's how I see it. Leaving him doesn't improve anything.

In the Quadrangle

REG. What do you do all day?

CATHY. There's nothing to do. Just sit about all day. Feel like running away.

REG. And the kids?

CATHY. Well, they're restless. They've had so many changes. I think it's strange to them, they wonder what's going to happen. It's no good. If you go out in the evening you have to be back at night by nine.

REG. What about eating?

CATHY. Well, there's potatoes.

REG. You never did like potatoes.

CATHY. The kids woke me up in the night. They were crying for bread.

The Same. Later

CATHY. I wish you would come more often, Reg.

REG. I can't afford to.

CATHY. You long for the night here sometimes. Not for sex like I used to.

The Same. Later

CATHY. Till all this happened, it was a happy marriage, weren't it, Reg?

REG. If it weren't for the kids, we wouldn't be here. Yeah, but I'm glad we had 'em. You can't wish your kids away.

CATHY. I wish we was starting all over again.

REG. I'd choose the same.

CATHY. Yes. I'd choose you, Reg. But now I want to look away.

The Big Room

MARLON *climbs into bed.* CATHY *tucks him up.* INMATE THREE *undresses* BRIAN.

INMATE. That your husband then?

CATHY. Yes.

INMATE. How long you been married then?

CATHY. Seven years.

INMATE. And what would be your husband's profession?

CATHY. He's not in work now.

She busies herself about the bed.

The Big Room

MRS. HARPY *and a guitar.*

MRS. HARPY. Not long now. At least, I don't think so. I'm practising very hard now and I'm hoping that soon a little bit of recognition may come my way, and with it a little lolly. This is an auto-harp actually. Shirley Abigail effect. I know my age is against me, I know that, but I'm in the hopes that we'll win through. Eh, Rudolph.

She picks up the guitar and strums a chord.

I'm on the track of something good now. We should be out of here soon.

We hear the voice of;

CATHY. It did go through me mind then to chuck the whole thing, turn my back on the kids and go off.

I felt I'd failed them. I knew they wasn't fit to be in a place like that. I thought how I used to be before we was married, without anyone depending on me, and had money in me pockets and some good times.

In the Big Room

CATHY *and the* KIDS.

CATHY. Once upon a time there were some kids and they lived with their mum whose name was Cathy.

In the Quadrangle

CATHY. Go Reg. Why don't you? You need a job, love. I heard there's jobs up there too. When you've got a job, you can find us a home there. It's easier up there, they say.

REG. That's what I thought, Cath. I will, love. I'll get a place up there for us.

CATHY. *Lying.* And then, soon the Smithson Estate will be finished. No more worries then.

REG. That's good. Well, if I haven't got anything fixed up there, I'll be back by then. Should be. But I should have something fixed up. Reg'll fix it.

MARLON *begins crying.*

The voice of;

CATHY. It was all strange. Because kids do seem, I dunno, when you consider it, they do seem to need some sort of feeling for their parents, like to look forward to their Dad as well as their Mum, to have a lark, their Dad as well as their Mum.

A Street

REG *crosses a street and disappears into the traffic.*

The Big Room

CATHY. Wasn't you the one brought my friend's baby back from the hospital? Weren't you? Brought it back from the hospital? Didn't you see then that it was still sick? Didn't you see then that it was still sick? Didn't you? Didn't you see?

MATRON. There was nothing to see. There was nothing wrong with the child. It was only in the hospital because of an abscess. It was in tip-top medical condition.

CATHY. If it was in tip-top medical condition then, how come it's dead now?

MATRON. The mother can't have looked after it properly dear. It must be the mother's fault.

CATHY. You accusing my friend?

MATRON. I'm stating the truth. The way some of you women keep your children . . .

CATHY. You! You're a cow!

The row continues and CATHY *strikes the* MATRON.

In the Warden's Office

The WARDEN *has a newspaper in his hand.*

WARDEN. I wonder who said this? You see it's about this place. I wonder who told these lies?

CATHY. It wasn't me.

WARDEN. Listen, young lady, I'm not as stupid as I may look. It was a blonde wasn't it who talked to the reporter? A blonde like you?

CATHY. I dunno who it was.

WARDEN. We've had some other reports about you I think. Yes, to do with Mrs. Selby.

CATHY. I was just telling her about the poor little baby that died.

ANOTHER MEMBER. Er, Mrs. Ward, I see that your husband hasn't been paying the fees.

CATHY. Paying the fees. He certainly has.

WARDEN. We would know if he was or wasn't.

CLERK. Didn't he tell you he wasn't paying?

CATHY. I didn't see him. Not for him to be able to.

CLERK. Didn't you see him? When did you last see your husband?

CATHY. *In shame.* Not for a while now.

CLERK. What's going on then young lady? Are you married or aren't you?

CATHY *loses her temper now. She cries;*

Shut up! Shut up!

WARDEN. You may go.

CATHY. Runts! You bleeding runts! I'll sod your rotting garments into runting garters for you. Runts! Runts!

The CLERK *guides her out.*

CATHY *weeps.*

The Big Room

CATHY *is reading a letter. 'Private and Confidential'. Dear Madam, It has now been decided that you should be required to vacate the temporary accommodation provided for you and your children on or before 31st October. It must be clearly understood that the temporary accomodation will no longer be available after that date.' What does it mean?*

INMATE *knows but she hasn't the strength to say.*

INMATE. Well, I don't know really.

INMATE. Shouldn't worry darling.

INMATE. Nothing to worry about.

CATHY *knows what it means.*

The Streets

In the days that follow CATHY *trudges the streets again with the* KIDS *trailing after her, forlornly putting coins in the telephone, making last appeals to friends she once had, even trying to contact* REG, *once more calling at house agents and scanning notice boards.*

Outside a Lodging House

CATHY. It's about a room.

LANDLADY. Yes dear. How many of you are there?

CATHY. There's just me and the two kids.

The Warden's Office

WARDEN. Don't be a fathead when your time's up. Don't be like Mr. Growcott. Let us take them away without making a fuss.

CATHY. What right have you got to take my kids from me?

WARDEN. You can't find a place for them can you? Well, you've had your chance. We're not interested in you now. It's the kids. We can't have them sleeping out. From the moment they leave here they'll be in need of care and protection.

The Big Room

CATHY *packing their few remaining garments into a carrier bag, including the carbunkle mirror.*

CATHY. Marlon and Mavis are going tomorrow.

MARLON. Where are we goin' to live now Mum, then?

CATHY. .....

MARLON. Mum, where we goin' to live now?

CATHY. .....

On the Road

They are walking, getting tired.

In a Park

At mid day she buys them some ices and teas in the nearby park.

In the Park. Later

Dusk comes early and it sees her and the children wandering through the mists of the park. But it is too cold to stay here.

As it grows dark she comes down from the park.

A Phone Box

Once more she tries to get hold of REG, *putting valuable money into the phone box. But there is no answer at the last humber he'd given her.*

A Large Station. Evening

CATHY *buys a cup of tea and some individual pies.*

Until midnight no one disturbs them—they could be waiting for a train. She sits, the CHILDREN*'s heads on her lap, one hand on each. Waiting. She has no more plans.*

The lights begin to go out in the mammoth station.

TWO MEN *approach her. They ask a few questions. One walks off and the* OTHER *stays by her. But she hasn't got the energy now to move on any more.*

The FIRST MAN *has nodded to* TWO WOMEN *round the corner. Now they are approaching.*

MAN. We don't want you. It's the children. Will you come with them in the car, to see the children safely installed? Would you like to come as far as the hostel?

CATHY. No, I'm not coming. And you're not taking my children.

WOMAN. In that case–

Each of the TWO WOMEN *puts one hand on each of the* TWO CHILDREN. *Then* CATHY *is filled with some fund of energy that she hadn't known she still had. She is like an animal now, fighting for them. And they overpower* CATHY *and the* CHILDREN *are carried off.*

CATHY. Don't cry . . . don't cry . . .

One of the MEN *asks* CATHY *if she'd like to go to a hostel and* CATHY *says;*

CATHY. No, I'm all right.

CATHY *goes to the 'All-Nite T Bar' and spends her last fourpence on a cup of tea.*

High over the spindly roof of the station a moon is rising.

The break-up of one family by our society is complete, and CATHY *walks out of the station.*

By the Clearway. Night

CATHY *is waiting for a lift.*

We see the following captions:

> *All the events in this film happened in Britain in the last eighteen months.*
>
> *Four thousand children each year are separated from their parents because they are homeless.*
>
> *West Germany has built twice as many houses as we have since the war.*

THE STORY BROUGHT UP TO DATE

Cathy Come Home was written ten years ago but, with a few exceptions, it is as true today as it was then.

When *Cathy* was written there was little information available in print. Now there is a lot. And there seems no end to Britain's housing crisis.

When *Cathy* was first transmitted the uproar concerning Britain's homeless families caused me to believe that there would be change.

Yet, in spite of all that public uproar, in spite of the fact that a social injustice of which the general public had previously been ignorant was now identified; in spite of the pledges of all parties to solve the housing crisis, and a specific Labour pledge to build 500,000 houses a year, what actually happened?

As Des Wilson has written, in a moving passage in his book 'It was the Places Fault': 'My guess is that for all the hullabaloo, Cathy is still homeless. Because, for all the hullabaloo, the emergency end of Britain's housing problem is worse. In 1966, for instance, there were 12,411 people in hostels for the homeless. In 1969 there were 18,849.' (The present total is 32,292).

'Greater numbers of casualties can be blamed on greater scarcity—in 1966 there were, for instance, 150,000 families on local authority waiting lists in London. In 1969 there were 190,000. (The present total is 238,000).

'It's possible that Cathy never saw her husband Reg and her three children Mylene, Marlon and Mavis again. It's possible that the children are among the 7,000 odd, who will tonight toss and turn in the beds of our children's homes—what we call 'in care'—for one reason only—their family haven't a decent home. The bewildered children of beaten parents.

'Most probably Cathy and Reg and the children did come back together again, but now struggle to survive as a family in an overcrowded and squalid slum. Homeless by any civilised definition. . . Cathy, still in her twenties, will already look old. She'll be apathetic and lethargic. Her skin will be unhealthy, and her nerves will be raw. . .

'As a nation, we are nearly always at the foot of the Western European League tables for expenditure on housing. We've never given housing that priority it deserves, and *Cathy* made no difference to that. As individuals, we never wanted to hear the cries for help before *Cathy* , and even now we prefer to hear the strident voice of prejudice against the homeless, than to accept the sacrifices we must make to save them.'

A recent report by Shelter revealed that the same sort of iniquities are still taking place in homes for the homeless as those described in *Cathy*. Bed and breakfast places are now frequently being used as alternatives to Part III Accommodation, at vast expense to the tax-payer; thousands of children are still being taken into care each year for no reason other than homelessness; and one hundred families apply for emergency accommodation every day.

When will we as a nation ever learn?

When, finally, will we actually get round to changing our legislation, our priorities, so that this tragic situation becomes a thing of the past?

Jeremy Sandford

BIBLIOGRAPHY

Allaun, Frank. *No Place Like Home.* Andre Deutsch (1972)

Berry, Fred. *Housing–The Great British Failure.* (1974).

Donnison, David D. *The Government of Housing.* Penguin (1967)

Glastonbury, B. *Homeless near a ThousandHomes.* Allen & Unwin (1972)

Greve, J. Page D., Greve, S. *Homelessness in London.* Scottish Academic Press, (1972) (x)

Harvey, Audrey. *Casualties of the Welfare State.* Fabian Pamphlet (1960)

HMSO. *Housing in Britain.* (1970).

Murie, Alan; Niner, Christopher; Watson, Pat. *Housing Policy and the Housing System.* George Allen and Unwin. (1976).

Rose, Hilary. *The Housing Problem.* Heineman Educational Books Ltd. (1968).

Shelter. *The Grief Report.* (1972); *Bed and Breakfast.* (1974).

Turner, John F.C. *Housing by People.* Marion Boyars. (1976).

Wilson, Des. *It Was the Place's Fault.'* Oliphants (1970).

FILMS

'*What Can be Done*'. Shelter (1974).

'*Cathy Come Home*'. The film of *Cathy* can be hired from Shelter, 86 Strand, London WC2, or from Concord Film Council Ltd., Ipswich, 1P10052.

ORGANISATIONS AND PRESSURE GROUPS

Shelter: 86 Strand, London, WC2.

Family Squatting Advisory Service: Blackfriars Settlement, 44 Nelson Square, London, SE1.

Rights against Homelessness: 1 Money's Yard, London, SW3